I0593379

STAR WARRIORS

MY ALIEN MATES BOOK 1

MAGGIE ALABASTER

Copyright © 2021 by Maggie Alabaster

All rights reserved.

No part of this book may be reproduced in any form or by any electronic or mechanical means, including information storage and retrieval systems, without written permission from the author, except for the use of brief quotations in a book review.

Edited by Lily Luchesi

Proofread by Nora Hogan

Cover by Atra Luna Designs

To the readers, I wish health and happiness.

MY FIRST TIME seeing Earth from the window of a space shuttle freaked me the fuck out.

I mean, who wouldn't be scared? I'd spent the last twenty two and a half years on the rock. It was home and I was going a long way away. So far, I could barely wrap my head around it.

"Are you o-okay?" A voice with a hint of a stammer broke through my uneasy thoughts.

I turned and forced a nervous smile, which probably looked like I needed to pee.

The guy who spoke was absolutely gorgeous. He was also blue. I don't mean he was cold either. His skin was steel blue, with a slight sheen that almost looked metallic. He was definitely not from Earth, but his brown-green eyes were surprisingly like a human's in shape and colour. Right now, they were locked on me. He seemed concerned, even anxious.

I met his gaze and my stomach fluttered. Nerves. It was just nerves. Yet the fluttering continued and I struggled to look away.

He cocked his head and I realised I hadn't responded.

I cleared my throat and willed my stomach to stop behaving like a silly teen. Hot guys like this didn't go for girls like me.

"I was thinking about," I swallowed down a knot of emotion, "leaving Earth." The last word choked out, as though saying it might make all of this more real.

I glanced out the window—or was it a porthole—and caught a glimpse of the edge of Africa. My breath caught in my throat. I blinked away a tear.

"I suppose that is a lot t-to think about." He looked down at his booted feet and shifted in his seat.

I wiped away a tear and took a moment to get a good look at him. Apart from his skin, he didn't seem that different to me. He was around the same age, with the short hair and the uniform of the military arm of the IF—The Interstellar Federation. A badge pinned to his chest marked him as an ensign.

"Yeah, it really is," I agreed. A whole hells of a lot.

He lifted the side of his face and looked at me with one eye. "I'm sorry, I'm not good with— with—"

"Aliens?" I suggested lightly. I probably looked as strange to him as he did to me.

He shook his head. "Conversation," he said finally. "Talking is…" A darker shade of blue crept up his cheeks.

"Difficult?" I said.

He nodded vigorously. "Yes. I could have been an ensign sooner, but I'm…" His head jerked up and his eyes widened apologetically. "I'm sorry. Here you are, leaving your home planet, and I'm babbling on."

"It's all right," I assured him quickly. "You're helping to take my mind off things. Stuff. Everything." *Very eloquent,* I told myself. "I'm Edie. Short for Edith." I grimaced. My parents were big fans of history and older style names. My brothers Julius and Horatio were even less lucky than I was, except in the middle name department. Mine was a closely guarded secret. Yes, it's that bad.

I held out my hand.

He stared at it, brow furrowed. "I'm sorry, I'm not sure what…"

"Oh." I realised the reason for his confusion. "You're supposed to shake it. It's an Earth thing, I suppose." I shrugged. I was about to pull my hand back when he gripped it and shook it so hard I thought my wrist might tear away from the rest of my arm. He stopped still and held on to my hand for longer than necessary.

"Not like that," I said. I gave an awkward laugh, although to sit like this, hand in hand, felt natural, like we'd done it a hundred times before.

My face heated.

His mouth formed an O and he released my hand like it was too hot.

"I'm sorry," he said for the third time in as many minutes. "I barely passed alien etiquette."

"It's okay." My skin tingled. "Plenty of humans wouldn't pass human etiquette. Here, let me show you." It was *totally* for educational purposes, not because I wanted to hold his hand again. Or so I told myself. I ignored the fluttering which now felt like backflips in my belly.

I held out my hand, but this time when he gripped it in his, I shook it gently.

"Just like that, see?" Oh yes, purely *educational*. So why did my stomach feel as if an impromptu dance-off was taking place in there?

He smiled, showing two rows of even, white

teeth. "This is called the sh-shaking of hands." He seemed very pleased with himself.

I chuckled. "Something like that." I took back my hand regretfully. "What's your name?"

"Danec, son of Jaec," he declared. He glanced down at his palm, a smile on his lips.

"Where are you from, Danec, son of Jaec?"

"Freytauri, a few st-stars over." He jerked his head in what I suspected was the wrong direction.

I smiled. "Is it nice there?"

"Nicer than Earth," he replied. His jaw dropped and he looked mortified. "I mean, um, it's just…"

I laughed silently and held up my fingers, my hand bent backward at the knuckles. "It's okay. I am leaving for a reason." A good reason, but that didn't make this any easier. I lowered my fingers and sighed. "They say Earth was lovely once."

"Before pollution, war, and the climate made it harder to live there," he said as though reading from a vidscreen. "I came top of my class in history." He puffed out his chest and for the first time I really noticed the bulge of muscle under his shirt. From what I've heard, the training with the IF was rigorous.

"Where are you headed?" he asked.

I glanced down at my watch. "I'm making a stop at the Moon Station for a night, then on to Agus."

Danec's face lit up. "Me too. Are you joining the GASP?" The Galactic Armed Space Force.

I hesitated. "I don't think I'm military material. I trained as a nurse, but my knowledge of alien—I mean, non-human biology is limited. I've heard the medical training facility on Agus is the best in the IF. After that, I'm not sure what I'll do."

"It is the best," Danec agreed. "I might see you around then." He looked hopeful. The expression made him even hotter, if that was possible.

"I'd like that," I said softly. "Can I ask you a question?"

"I..." He blinked and his shyness returned. "I suppose so."

I chewed my lip for a moment. "Is everyone from Freytauri blue?"

"Oh," he looked relieved. What had he expected me to ask? "Yes, we are. Although some tend toward purple. Some confuse us with the Agusians because we look similar, but they tend toward green. We share a common ancestor with them and the people of Earth—" He stopped, eyes wide. "I'm babbling again."

"Not at all," I said. "It's nice to see someone so passionate about things."

He blushed again. "My friends called me a gwarp, because I like to read and learn."

I bit back a laugh, in case he thought it was directed at him. "A gwarp? Is that like a nerd or a geek?"

"Or a dork," he said. "Human slang is fascinating."

"Oh I don't know, Freytaurian is pretty interesting too, by the sound of it."

He cocked his head. "We have fewer words for toilet and penis than humans do." He said 'penis' like he'd said 'arm' or 'leg.' Just another body part, nothing to be embarrassed about.

I liked that.

"I'm not even slightly surprised," I said ruefully. "Humans have long been obsessed with both of those things." Not that I could talk. I enjoyed toilet humour and cocks as much as the next girl.

"We have many words for stars and hard work." The side of his mouth quirked up. "I suppose our culture has different priorities."

I laughed again. "You could say that." Apparently ours was all about the groin area. No wonder the planet was a mess.

I looked out the window and sighed, as did several other humans who sat in the seats behind me. The shuttle was small, only big enough for a hundred people, but it moved fast enough that I could already see almost the whole side of Earth. Mostly blue, the continents stood out as the only landmasses still above water. The rest were gone some fifty years ago, before I was born. Old footage shows islands dotting the ocean, full of life and odd trees called palms. Agus had islands. With any luck, I'd get to see one.

"I remember the first time I left Freytauri," Danec said softly. "I was nervous too. I was worried I would never return."

Without looking away from the window, I asked, "Did you?"

"A few months later, yes, for the equinox festival. It's an old tradition on Frey-T, as we call it. Some think it's silly to keep celebrating it. It goes back to times when we believed in gods and demons."

I glanced over to him and nodded. "Some humans still believe in those things, but we have celebrations that go back a long time, too. Christmas, for example."

"Ah. Turkey and a man in red who fits down a—" He paused and looked uncertain. "Chimney?"

I smiled. "Something like that. Don't tell me, you didn't ace Earth ceremonies."

"Uh." He rubbed his smooth chin. "Earth ceremonies only takes up half a page in the book about galactic traditions."

I sniffed. "I think I should be offended we're not considered more interesting."

"Oh, microns," he swore under his breath. If you can call that swearing. "I didn't mean to offend you. The IF knows comparatively little about your culture and it takes a while for them to start to teach them. They spend m-more time talking more about updating the syllabus than doing it. Or s-so my teachers say."

"It's okay." Without thinking, I took his hand and gave it a squeeze. "I'm not really upset. Everywhere else seems more interesting than Earth."

He looked down at our hands until I felt uncomfortable and drew mine back.

"Please tell me that didn't mean something rude on Frey-T," I said tentatively.

He looked surprised. "Not at all. It's considered intimate."

"As in sexual?" I felt my face heat.

"Oh no," he said quickly. "Like two people who

MAGGIE ALABASTER

care for each other. If you had laced your little finger into mine, that might be construed as, um..."

"Yes?" I prompted. "As what?"

"As you wishing to have sex with me." He blushed.

"Oh, I see. that's good to know." It really was. A girl didn't want to get herself into trouble accidentally. On purpose, well that was another story, but we had just met. He seemed cute and sweet. Okay, a little hot too, but ten minutes was too soon to jump into anything with someone, no matter the size of his biceps.

"I'll be sure to keep my hands to myself from now on," I said. "Just in case I do something wrong."

"Yes." He grimaced. "I don't mind. Most people understand—well, have misunderstandings, but some get offended easily."

I knitted my brows slightly. "You seem to be referring to something in particular."

He exhaled and lowered his voice. "Some of the folk from Parvora 12 can be cranky. A few of the trainers on Agus are from there and they..." He inhaled through his nose. "Most of the cadets and ensigns are terrified of them."

"So they're assholes?" I suggested.

Danec looked confused. "Oh, you mean they

aren't very nice. You used body parts to say that?"

I grinned. "Like I said, we're obsessed with that area of the human body. Dickhead, asshole, butthead, wanker..."

Danec looked even more confused. "Isn't that last one another word for masturbation?" Just as he spoke, silence fell across the shuttle and his words seemed to echo through the cabin.

Several dozen eyes turned to Danec and several people snickered.

"Yes, it is," I said, my voice softer than his. "It's considered something people don't talk about in the open. Is it different on Frey-T?"

He shrugged. "It is as talked about as any other act of sex, which is to say not much. It's not considered strange or shameful."

"Right. But you wouldn't do it in public?" Wonderful, now I was imagining him doing just that, his hand wrapped around his throbbing...

Gods, stop it, Edie, before you leave a puddle on the seat.

Danec turned darker blue than ever. "Oh, microns no. It's an intimate thing."

"We really aren't so different," I said. I couldn't help but wonder what our similarities were, biologically speaking. I eyed his groin. He did seem to have a bulge there, like a human guy, but that didn't necessarily mean it resembled a human cock.

"So, um... Do they feed us on board the shuttle?" I was hungry now, but not necessarily for food. Although, I could eat if it was offered. If, that was, my stomach would stop with the acrobatics.

"Uh." He tongue slid over his lips and I suspected he was thinking along the same lines as I was. Not about food, about other things, like intimacy. "The ride is short and the shuttle has no galley. But Moon Station has a large mess."

"I'm sure it does." I chuckled. 'Large mess' sounded like anywhere I stayed for more than a few days. I saved cleanliness for work.

Danec cleared his throat. "Would you like to ha-have..." He looked frustrated at his own stammer. "Have dinner with me?"

"I'd like that." When I'd stepped onto the shuttle, I hadn't expected to make a friend, much less dinner plans, but why not embrace it? My old life was disappearing in the window at the back of the shuttle, I should grab the new one by the balls and enjoy the fuck out of it.

That didn't stop another sigh from escaping my lips as the Earth turned and Australia passed under us. It too had islands around it once.

2

―――――――――

"CAN YOU BELIEVE THIS PLACE?" The voice who spoke was female, but it took me a few moments to realise she was talking to me.

I turned from staring out the Moon Station window. "I suppose I can't."

She was shorter than me, but more slender. Her pale hair was swept back in a neat ponytail, with no strands escaping from anywhere. Absently I patted my own hair, but my dark curls wouldn't be tamed, no matter how hard I tried. I have the kind of hair people claim they wish they had, but those of us who did, spent hours detangling it with a hairbrush and a straightener.

"It's mind-blowing," she declared. "We can see the

whole Earth from here. Well, the bit that's facing us. Look, North America. I'm Brinley Grant."

She slipped in her name so quickly I almost missed it.

"Hi. Edie." I put down my cup of coffee onto the table in front of me and offered my hand.

She shook it and slipped into the seat opposite me.

"Where are you from?" she asked. "Obviously Earth. Me too. I'm from the south of England."

I had figured that from her accent. "Australia," I said while she took a breath. "Sydney, specifically."

"Oh, fabulous. I watched that go past on the last rotation. It's amazing to see water where there wasn't water for hundreds of years." She must have seen the expression on my face, because she stopped speaking.

"I'm terribly sorry. My mouth runs away from me at times. A lot of the time, actually."

"It's okay," I said quickly. "We need to think of ourselves as citizens of the IF now, not just Earth." It was a simple thing to say, but to do, that was something else.

"Yes. Or Agus. You're going there too, aren't you?" Brinley asked. "I checked the manifest. Oh, don't worry, I wasn't spying. I'm training to fly the shut-

tles. I'm hoping to fly the bigger space transports."
She smiled like a child whose dreams had all come
true. Or were about to.

"That sounds like fun." I tried to seem enthusias-
tic, but I'd never had much affinity with machinery.

"Doesn't it?" she agreed. "There's nothing like
flying. I started with small planes when I was
younger and—" She rattled on while I watched the
world go by.

"So, why are you going to Agus?" she asked.

When I told her, she all but bounced in her chair.
"It's good to know I would be in good hands if I got
sick," she said.

"You might be," I replied modestly. "I mean, I do
my best." I loved my job and knew I did it well, but I
might be out of my depth dealing with other species.

I watched two women walk past the table. One,
who I assumed was from Frey-T, had skin lighter
than Danec and dark, pin-straight hair. The green-
skinned woman from Agus had antennas and scales
across her chest and up the sides of her neck. Both
were slender and taller than me.

"They're beautiful, aren't they?" Brinley said
softly. "I wish I was that tall. And thin."

I pursed my lips. Even the prettiest amongst us
was unhappy about some aspect of ourselves. Did

the aliens feel the same way? Was 'alien' even the right word? We were as alien as they were.

IF, I reminded myself. *We're all IF.*

"From what I know of their physiology, they have narrower, longer bones," I said. "We couldn't look like that if we tried. Besides, if you were too tall, you wouldn't fit into the cockpit." I was guessing, but cockpits always seemed small to me.

Apparently it was the right thing to say, because she smiled.

"That's true, but if I was any shorter, I wouldn't touch the floor while sitting in a pilot's chair either."

"I'm sure you would find a way," I assured her. She didn't seem like the kind of woman who let a thing like height stop her from doing what she wanted.

"Yes, I suppose I would," she said thoughtfully. "Did you know there isn't any meat on the Moon Station? Apart from human meat, that is."

I wasn't sure if I should feel whiplashed from the sudden change of topic, or sickened at the idea of people being meat. Maybe both.

I shook my head. "I suppose it's hard to farm up here, apart from grains and vegetables."

"Exactly. The amount of oxygen it would take to support a herd of cattle would be prohibitively expensive. That also means the milk in your coffee is plant based."

"Most of the IF doesn't farm animals," I said. "Most other worlds find the eating of flesh to be..."

"Yucky?" she suggested.

"Yes, yucky. Luckily they like coffee and chocolate as much as we do." The introduction of those two things to the IF might be Earth's greatest contribution, which was kinda lame. At least we contributed *something*.

"I'm not sure I would have left Earth if there wasn't chocolate out there," Brinley said with a cheeky smile.

I chuckled. "Me either." A girl had to have some vices and I had several, but chocolate was the biggest one.

"Maybe we can share a cabin on the ship to Agus?" Brinley suggested.

"That would be nice," I said. I didn't want to be the kind of person who left home and only congregated with my own kind, but leaving Earth was a huge deal and having another human close by would help ease us both into this new life.

"Great, I'll sort it out." She glanced at something behind me. "In the meantime, that guy from Frey-T.

I don't think he's taken his eyes off you since I sat down."

I swivelled in my seat in time to see Danec look away, his cheeks flushed.

"Oh. We met on the shuttle up," I said. He really was pretty adorable. He looked back for a second and blushed darker.

"We're supposed to go out to dinner tonight." I offered him a smile and turned back to Brinley.

"But?" she prompted.

"But there are so many women on the station who are more interesting than I am," I finished with a sigh. "And prettier." Slimmer. Taller.

I would understand if he changed his mind.

"Bollocks," Brinley said loudly. "You're very interesting. If you weren't, he wouldn't have asked you, would he?"

I gaped for a moment, surprised at the force of her reply. "I suppose not."

"Exactly, and look, he's coming over here."

I just took a sip of coffee and now I almost choked on it. I coughed and swallowed as hastily as I could and put my cup back down.

"Watch where you're going." A human man, a scowl on his features, all but pushed Danec out of the way as he made his way past.

"I-I'm sorry," Danec stammered. "I-I didn't—"

"Stupid prick," the man muttered, loud enough for me to hear.

"Prick," Danec said loudly, his eyes bright. "That's another word for penis, isn't it? You humans really are obsessed with the groin area."

The man, a badge on his chest read 'Jones,' glared at Danec and stomped away.

I put a hand over my mouth as he passed, to stifle a laugh.

Danec watched him leave, confusion on his face. "Was it something I said.?"

I couldn't hold back any longer. I laughed until tears leaked down my cheeks.

Danec looked bewildered all the while.

"It's all right." I wiped my eyes with my sleeve and rose to pat him on the shoulder. "Some humans don't like to be reminded of our obsession."

"And some people are just cranky," Brinley said. "I met him on the shuttle up. He really didn't want to leave Earth."

I immediately felt bad for laughing at him. We were all in this together, or at least we should be. Later, I might seek him out, to see if he was okay, but I would give him time to calm down first.

"Do you still want to have dinner with me?" Danec asked. He gave me a shy, uncertain smile.

Those backflips in my stomach were back. I'm sure it was a coincidence they happened whenever he spoke to me.

My mouth was suddenly dry, but I managed to say, "Yes. I'm looking forward to it." I moistened my lips with my tongue and added, "I feel like maybe I should tell you all the groin-related words and when to avoid using them."

"I would welcome any education you could give me." He nodded vigorously, eyes wide with excitement.

"Lucky girl," Brinley murmured.

I glanced at her and blushed. I didn't think that was what he meant. At least, I was *almost* sure.

"Um, so I'll meet you back here in..." I pulled up my sleeve so I could see the face of my watch. "Two hours?"

"Yes." He checked his own watch, a newer version of mine. He must have some credits if he could afford it. Not that I cared about his credit account balance. He was sweet and seemed genuine. And the trapeze in my belly must mean *something*.

"I should go," he said regretfully. "I have to catch up on my studies."

"Three cheers for free, intergalactic internet," I said, if only to keep him there a few moments longer. The internet was still used for the same things it had always been used for: studying, cat videos, and porn. These days the cats were more interesting, like the Parvoran cheetah, with its two tails and distinctive purr. And the Blarvian Watercat, with their gills and fishlike tail.

The porn, well I'd never been one to partake. I preferred to make my own experiences. Which brought me back to the present moment.

Danec's eyes lingered on mine before he smiled and turned away.

"He has a cute ass and everything." Brinley sighed. "Can you ask if he has a brother?"

"I'm sure there will be plenty of guys on Agus," I assured her. "Or girls. Or whatever you're into." The IF was diverse in ways humans wouldn't have imagined a hundred years ago. Some worlds had multiple genders. Some, like Blarvius, had the reproductive abilities of males and females, so they could have their own children if they wanted to. A handy skill, I guess.

"I'm into people with brains," Brinley replied firmly. "And a sense of humour. It wouldn't hurt if they just happen to be cute as well. Danec certainly is."

"That he is," I agreed. And he wanted to share dinner with me. *Me*.

"I suppose I should shower and start getting ready," I said uncertainly. How seriously should I take this? Fancy hair, makeup, and everything, or casual and without too many expectations? Oh, who was I kidding, it would take me two hours to untangle my hair. I should start on that right now.

And think about what to wear.

And—

"Do you want some company while you get ready?" Brinley asked. "I just got the latest episodes of *Darker Side of Parvora* on IF-View."

I managed to hold back a squeal. "That's my favourite show. Right along with *The Real Domewives of Garvi-3.*"

Brinley snorted and offered me her arm. "You know none of that is real, right?"

"Of course, but that's half the fun." Really, if I had that many credits in my account, I'd probably find more useful things to do with my time, but it was just a Vid show.

"It's definitely better than *Keeping Up With the*

Centaurians." Did people really believe what went on on that show?

"That's true," Brinley agreed. "Can you believe some people dyed their skin yellow, just to look like them? Folks do the strangest things."

I laughed and walked out of the mess hall with her. Just outside, the station opened out into a large space that led to the hangar. Across on the other side, a sulky figure stood alone. Jones turned and looked at me as though his eyes might pierce a hole. Nothing about him suggested he'd welcome a chat from me, even if I was just being nice.

I looked back, my gaze unwavering, until we moved into the corridor which led to the living quarters. I put him out of my mind as best I could, but I felt as though his gaze was bored into my skin.

3

"IF WE WERE ON EARTH, I would ask you where you wanted to go," Danec said. "Or what you wanted to eat. There's not much to choose from here. It's the mess or the mess."

"Hmmm, let me think about that for a moment." I twirled a curl around my finger. "How about the mess?"

He laughed, awkward and high. "Great idea." He drew his shoulders in like a shy schoolboy, and added, "You look lovely, by the way."

"You too," I replied. "I mean, handsome." Trust me to put my foot in my mouth. Not literally, of course, these were my favourite heels. Okay, my only heels. The luggage weight limit meant I had to leave the other dozen pairs behind. My parents promised to take care of them and send them on when I was settled, along with my collection of earrings shaped like food. What? Who doesn't need earrings shaped like purple gummy bears, or vodka bottles?

He really was handsome though. His blue skin had a subtle sheen in the station's lights. His short hair was damp around the edges and he smelled clean, like he'd just come from the shower. His uniform was neat and fit like it was cut just for him, firm across his chest and biceps. I was tempted to ask him to do a twirl, just so I could see how it fit his ass. What I saw was pretty damned good.

"The mess it is then," he said. "I heard they're thawing pizza tonight."

I wrinkled my nose. "Mmm, thawed pizza." The resources here on the station were limited and the galley was relatively small, even if the mess could seat a few hundred people. So frozen food it was, much of the time, usually prepared on Earth.

"It's better than fish sticks." He stuck out his tongue in disgust. "I had that on the way through. I don't think it was real fish."

"They can put a station on the moon, but they still can't make decent fish sticks," I said.

Danec chuckled. "Yes. Um." He looked toward his booted feet.

"Shall we start walking?" I suggested. "Otherwise the mess might close before we get there."

"Right!" he said so quickly he seemed to startle himself. "I mean yes, good idea." He sighed. "I'm sorry, I don't mean to be awkward." He walked beside me. "My mother hoped being an ensign might make me more, um..."

"Confident?" I suggested.

"Exactly. Even with the uniform on, I feel as though I'm going to fall over my own feet."

"I'm sure you're not," I assured him. "You look very dashing. That shade of grey suits you."

I supposed I would have to wear a uniform too, once I boarded the ship to Agus. All the more reason to enjoy wearing a black skater skirt and a pale pink top. Both would probably look better on Brinley, but I felt cute in them.

"Thank you. You're very sweet."

Sweet? That sounded like a friend zone word right there. For some reason, my heart sank a little, but it was okay, really. Who couldn't use more friends? Especially when travelling to a whole new planet? If he just wanted friendship, then that's what we'd do.

"I try," I said, suddenly as awkward as he was. "There's an empty table, over near the window." If we ran out of things to talk about, we could always watch the world go by.

"Yes, great." He barrelled toward it like a man on a mission, almost leaving me standing at the entrance.

I raised my eyebrows at his back and hurried to catch up. At least I got a good view of his ass. It was everything I hoped it would be.

"We got it." He smiled like a little boy who rode his bike alone for the first time. If little boys had muscles and a dimple in their chin. I hadn't noticed that before, but now I did, I found it endearing.

Friends, Edie, friends, I reminded myself. It's okay to think your friends are hot, right? Awkward or not, he was a pretty sexy guy. Of course, leave it to me to meet an adorable guy who wanted to be friends. I suck at this love thing.

I shook off my self pity and smiled. "Good work. We beat another couple of people to it as well."

A woman with a tray had headed straight for it, but she slumped down at another table instead.

Danec's face fell. "I hope we didn't upset anyone." He pulled out a chair and gestured for me to sit. "I read in etiquette class that human women always like someone to pull out a chair for them."

It was a gesture all but abandoned on Earth, in

favour of equality and all that, but I didn't have the heart to tell Danec that. Instead, I smiled and slid into the seat.

"Thank you, that's very gentlemanly of you."

He furrowed his brow. "Gentlemanly? You have some words which aren't related to the groin."

I snorted so loud the people at the next tables turned and stared. I ignored them.

"Yes, one or two," I agreed. "Some countries have lots of words for snow."

"Interesting," he said. He pulled out his own chair and went to sit, but caught himself at the last moment. "I should get us food." He shot back up so fast, he knocked into his chair. It skidded back into the one behind him, earning him a glare from its occupant.

"Um, sorry." He retrieved the chair, tucked it back under the table and hurried away. Eyes and chuckles followed him.

My gaze followed his ass. Brinley was right, it was as perfect an ass as I had ever seen.

Friends, friends, I reminded myself again. I focused my attention out the window at the twinkling lights of some city below. I couldn't tell where it was and truthfully I wasn't trying very hard. If I did, I might cry. I hadn't expected to feel homesick, but it crept up in me while I sat alone at the table. I almost gave in to tears when Danec plonked a plate in front of me, startling me out of my thoughts.

"I'm sorry, the plate got hot." Danec placed his down opposite me and blew on his fingertips.

"Did you burn yourself?" I asked. "Here, let me see." I held out my hand.

I examined his fingers closely, partly because it's my job and partly because I hadn't seen blue skin up this close before. Like humans, he had fingerprints, but they all looked like arches, rather than whorls or loops. Lines crossed his palms the same as they did mine. That was a no brainer. without those, he couldn't open and close them. Still, it intrigued me.

Without thinking, I traced the lifeline across his palm with my fingertip.

"Is it all right?" he asked. "Did I damage myself?"

"Hmmm? Oh." I almost dropped his hand when I realised what I was doing. "Yes. I mean no, everything seems fine. No burns that I can see." I hadn't expected to find any, or he would have been more distressed.

"That's great," he said. "Thank you, I feel much better having you look at it."

"Even if I'm not familiar with your physiology?" I asked. "You might have nerves in the skin I can't see."

He flexed his hand, then picked up a piece of pizza—for some reason they were cut into squares—and shrugged with his opposite shoulder. "It feels fine. I might even be able to play the, what do you call it, piano, some day."

"Oh, you play?" The pizza looked as though it was made out of spare sheets of cardboard, but it tasted okay.

"No, I've never been any good at music." He grinned.

I chuckled. "Being uninjured doesn't give you magical powers, my friend."

He seemed disappointed at something, but he didn't say anything other than to flash a vague smile and went on eating.

We ate in silence for the next few minutes. Every so often I glanced out the window. Clusters of light were interspersed with great expanses of blackness. Oceans, I supposed, or places too small to be visible from space.

"It's so dark compared to Frey-T," Danec said softly. "Everything is run on solar power, water and all of that, but there are more lights at night. Even the oceans are dotted with floating cities."

"It sounds pretty," I said.

"It is," he agreed. "Our population is a lot more

spread out, so everyone has privacy and room to—I'm babbling, aren't I?"

I smiled. "Not at all. I like to hear about other planets. I've only seen them on my vidscreen."

"Same, until I came here." He waved toward Earth. "Seeing it from the station, or a screen, and being there, are two different things."

"I suppose that's true." Seeing Earth from here made it look like any other planet. That thought sat so heavily on my chest it became difficult to breathe. I grabbed a cup from the tray in the centre of the table and poured myself a drink of water. I gulped it down so fast I almost choked.

"We call it The Yearning," Danec said softly. "When you're missing home. Do you have a groin related word for it?"

His joke took me by surprise. I started to laugh, but ended up snorting water out my nose.

"Shit," I said under my breath. I pulled a tissue out of my pocket and wiped my nose. "I'm sorry." He must have thought I was an absolute dork by now. No wonder he only wanted to be friends.

He sat with his head cocked, eyes wide. "Fascinating. Your nose leaked. Are you unwell?"

I held back another laugh. "I'm fine. It's a human

thing I guess. My eyes leak too, sometimes." I felt like they might right now.

"Oh, ours too. It keeps our eyes from becoming dry."

"You don't cry?" I asked. "With tears?" I leaned in and peered more closely. He had tear ducts, more or less like mine.

"We cry, but no excess water comes out."

"Oh, I see." I sat back and went on eating. I'd always felt like men came from another planet, this one actually did.

"I—"

I let out a squeak as an alarm pounded through the mess. I dropped my piece of pizza and looked around, frantically.

"All IF personnel report to their stations," a robotic voice said over the speakers. A trill sounded, following the announcement.

"A drill?" Danec said. "Now?" He sagged back in his chair and made a face.

My heart sank. "I suppose they want to keep everyone on their toes," I said. The timing sucked. Our date, if you can call it that, was awkward, but I was enjoying myself.

"I suppose so," he said. He shoved a mouthful of pizza into his mouth and washed it down with water, while the people around us scrambled to their feet.

"That includes you, ensign." A cold voice was followed by a shadow which fell over the table.

Eyes colder than his voice regarded Danec and me. Deep red eyes, almost black, narrowed as I stared back. His skin was a shade lighter than his eyes. No, I realised, it wasn't skin, he was covered in a fine layer of fur. At least, his face was. The rest was obscured by a uniform like Danec's, but somehow neater and with the rank insignia of commander on his chest.

Danec leapt to his feet. "Yes, sir. Sorry, sir." He saluted sharply. "At once, Commander J'avet." He shot me an apologetic look, which lingered a nanosecond longer that was necessary, before he hurried away at a trot.

J'avet's eyes locked on me like a heat seeking missile. Or a heat giving one. My heart raced and I might have smiled if I didn't get the sense he loathed me on sight. Okay, two can play at that game.

I didn't move, I didn't blink even though I needed to. I sat perfectly still like scared prey. Except the scared part. I wasn't scared at all, no way. Well, maybe a little bit. He was clearly the kind of man used to giving orders and having others jump at them.

Right when I was about to look away, he did first.

"If you're heading for Agus, you're also IF personnel. You should get to your station."

"Uh, yes, sir," I said without thinking.

Shit, he turned back and stared at me again, this time with a raised eyebrow. Technically, I didn't report to him, unless he was the head of the station, which I was sure he wasn't.

"Commander is adequate," he said in a voice deep enough to make me wonder where else he had fur.

I shook myself out of my silly thoughts and stood. It was unlikely I would find out, unless he was sick or injured. I wouldn't wish that on anyone, no matter their attitude toward me.

I gave him a nod. "Commander then," I said, and hurried away to the infirmary.

4

"WHAT WAS THAT ALL ABOUT?" Brinley set down her mug and flipped her plait over her shoulder.

"What was what about?" I sipped my coffee with its not-quite milk and wrinkled my nose. The more I drank, the more I could taste it. I shouldn't be drinking caffeine this close to bedtime anyway, but I hoped to bump into Danec, Brinley or even Commander J'avet. What can I say, I'm a glutton for punishment.

"The drill." She flopped into a chair and pulled her plait back to the front of her shoulder. "I got to the hangar, but it was over before we could even step foot on the shuttle. It was almost as though…"

"Someone just wanted to interrupt things?" I suggested. For some reason, my mind went to J'avet.

I dismissed the thought immediately. For one thing, why would he bother? For another, he undoubtedly had better things to do with his time.

I shrugged. "Maybe it's just a thing they do in the IF. Get everyone to jump up to see how fast they can get to their stations."

Brinley snapped her fingers. "That's probably it. I wonder how we did."

I remembered how slow Danec and I had been, and grimaced. "I would expect they'll test us all again soon." Next time we wouldn't let anyone else down.

Brinley placed her elbow on the table and leaned her head on her fist. "At least life won't be boring."

"That's true," I agreed, "but I hope they don't decide to run drills in the middle of the night."

I've done my share of night shifts, like any other nurse, but I hadn't slept much the night before. We'd had to turn up at the launch site yesterday morning. They'd put us through a health test and information sessions about what to expect on the shuttle and on Agus. We'd each had an individual assessment of our mental health as well. Most people saw a psychologist these days, for one thing or another, and no one so much as blinked. Mental health doesn't have the stigma it once did.

After the interviews, we were housed in a long

building, with a small room each. A handful of couples shared, or people who were friends already. The rest of us had a room to ourselves. Of course, the rooms were uncomfortable and sterile and the thrum of air conditioning kept me awake half the night. The couple in the next room kept me awake for the other half. Whoever 'babe' and sweet cheeks' were, they were vigorous and energetic. Lucky them.

"So, how was your date?" Brinley gave me a sly smile.

"Short and sweet," I said ruefully. Much like my last sexual encounter. "He just wants to be friends. I guess that's for the best. We'll both be busy for a long time." I debated whether or not I should mention the commander, when the man himself strode past. My eyes locked on him so hard I wasn't sure I could look away if I wanted to. Damn, the guy would make any woman wet.

Shit. He turned and his gaze fell on me. I would have called it smouldering, until he curled his lip at me.

Asshole.

"Who is that?" Brinley whispered loudly.

"No one," I replied firmly. I looked away and picked up my cup as if it was the most interesting thing in the world. I wanted to look back and see if he'd gone, but I didn't dare.

"No one is hot," Brinley said.

"I think he thinks he is." I sipped my coffee and tucked a stray curl behind my ear. It popped straight back out again.

I heard someone laugh and thought it came from J'avet's direction, but I ignored it.

"He either doesn't like humans or he doesn't like me," I said. Either way, I had no time for him, even if I could imagine his hands on my—

No, I told myself. Leave the attraction to jerks behind on Earth, where it belongs.

There, that was great advice I gave myself. I should start one of those blogs where people ask for advice on their love lives. Oh, who was I kidding? I'd make theirs worse and get tossed out an airlock.

"Jerks are everywhere," Brinley said with a nod.

"Yeah, all over the galaxy," I agreed. Our galaxy at least.

I finished my coffee and stretched my arms over my head. "I might turn in. We have a big day ahead of us."

"Right. Assuming the ship is on time, it should dock around nine am, station time," Brinley said.

"It'll be refuelled, cleaned, and ready to head back by two pm."

I was expected to board shortly after docking, to help clean the infirmary and to get my rosters. This was no free trip across the galaxy here. I was expected to work, as least as much as I could with unfamiliar species, for full shifts.

A flutter of nerves tickled the inside of my belly. Not the kind I felt when I spoke to Danec. Those were the size of Earth. This was the size of the moon. Maybe two moons. The possibility of messing up too badly was minimal, I would be watched closely every shift, but I was still going to be on an alien spaceship, headed for a whole new planet. It was the adventure of a lifetime, but it was terrifying.

"You'll be fine," Brinley said, as though she read my mind. She probably felt the same way I did. She seemed as nervous. "We'll take care of each other."

I nodded. "I'm glad we're traveling at the same time."

"Me too." She smiled softly. "I'm going to finish my coffee, then turn in."

"Night." I rose and covered a yawn as I dropped my cup in a bucket outside the galley and made my way out of the mess.

"You can't mean to consort with them?"

I hadn't seen Jones until he spoke. He stepped out of the shadows near the sleeping quarters, his eyes on me.

"Huh?" I was too tired for pleasantries right now. "Did you want something?"

He took his time to answer. "I want the aliens to back off Earth," he said finally. His voice was rough, gravelly.

I rubbed my forehead. "You're on a station on the moon. Aren't you headed to Agus too?"

He huffed. "Because I want to learn more about their power systems. They're better for the environment. I'm going to take that back to Earth. To make it better."

"That's admirable—" I started.

"Yeah. Then we won't need them anymore. Earth can stand on its own. They can fuck off where they came from."

A knot of anger stirred in my chest. "Is that what this is about? Good, old fashioned racism? I thought they'd stamped that out decades ago."

"I don't care what colour they are," he hissed. "I just want them gone from Earth. We don't need 'em, and here you are, having dinner with one, making eyes at another." He wore his dark hair in a low ponytail. He gripped it now and clenched his teeth until his face turned red.

"Are you stalking me?" I asked. That, unfortunately, hadn't been stamped out. Even with better mental health care, people slipped through the cracks, as they say.

He sighed and dropped his hands to his sides. "No, I just happened to see. You can't want Earth to become a colony of some other planet. We'll all end up slaves." He didn't sound delusional, just scared.

"The IF would never let that happen," I said.

"Let?" he echoed with a bitter laugh. "Once our minerals are gone, they won't care. They'll abandon us to..." He shook his head. "We can't let that happen."

"We won't," I said firmly. "Humans are badass, and other planets will help—"

"At what price?" he asked. "No one ever does anything for free. Ever."

That was true, but I wasn't going to be dragged into a debate right now. "Look, I'm tired."

"Just watch yourself," he hissed. "Don't trust any of the aliens. Be careful. Promise?"

I didn't owe him a thing. Perhaps he was unhinged after all. How had he passed the psych test?

"I promise I'll be careful," I said. That was an easy promise to make. I had no intention of getting injured, or anything else for that matter.

"Good." He nodded. "If you need help getting away from them, you only have to ask. I'll... I'll do something."

I didn't know what he might do, and I suspected he didn't either. I made a mental note to check his assessment when I boarded the ship in the morning. If anything strange stood out, I would speak to my supervisor. Before the ship left with Jones on board. He wouldn't thank me for getting him kicked off, but if he needed help, he should go back to Earth and get it.

"Thank you," I said awkwardly. "I'm sure I'll be fine. It's nice to, um, have someone watching my back."

He nodded, flashed me a smile which might have been charming at some other time, and turned and walked away.

I watched him through narrowed, confused eyes and gave my head a shake. Some of what he said made a lot of sense. Earth *could* use some more sustainable energy, and shouldn't become too reliant on other worlds. On the other hand, places like Agus and Frey-T had benefited from IF membership for over eighty years now. It wasn't perfect, no organisation was, but it did seem to help its member worlds more than it hindered them.

Unless, of course, he knew more about it than I did. That was entirely possible. I had spent the last few years studying and paying little attention to galactic politics.

"I should keep doing that," I said to myself. A couple walking past stopped to stare, but I flashed them a smile and kept on walking toward my accomodation. With any luck, I wouldn't be next to 'babe' and 'sweet cheeks' tonight. Or the walls here would be nice and thick. Very thick.

I found room seventy-one and slid the card into the slot beside it. Humanity had yet to find a better way to unlock doors. The door slid aside and I stepped in.

The room contained one wide bed, a small wardrobe, and a table. No scope for more than a night or two. I guess the moon didn't want too many people to overstay.

I stripped down to my underwear and tossed my clothes in the direction of the table. I preferred to sleep naked, but in the case of a sudden drill, I decided it would be better if I didn't. Running around the station naked was something I didn't want to do, if I could help it.

I slipped into bed, pulled the covers over myself, and let my mind wander. If I dreamed tonight, it would consist of red fur, blue skin, and conspiracy theories. Preferably the first two. Maybe separately, maybe not.

A girl could dream, right?

5

THE INFIRMARY onboard the *Infinity* was bigger than the one on the Moon Station. Unlike the station, this was designed for a few hundred people. I didn't want to think about what might cause it to be at capacity. Space battles *had* happened in the past. With any luck, they would stay in the past, but ships were still made fully equipped for just about anything.

In one corner, a curtain was closed around a bed, obscuring a patient. I craned my neck and tried to peer through a gap, but before I could, another medic entered.

She saw what I was doing and cleared her throat.

I jumped to attention, my face pink. "I'm sorry, um, Doctor." Her badge read, 'Kalvix'. I groaned to myself. Of course I'd make a fool of myself in front of the senior medic on the ship.

Kalvix was slightly taller than me. Her skin was the soft green of new leaves. Her dark hair was cut short, like a pixie. Her green eyes added to the effect of an ethereal forest creature, as did the line of scales which ran down her neck and disappeared under her IF tunic. Her antennae twitched, one in my direction, the other toward the curtain.

"Mmmm." Her lips pursed disapprovingly, but she didn't appear to be angry. "Nurse Wright, I assume."

"Yes," I said quickly. "It's nice to meet you." I wasn't sure if shaking hands was something done on Agus, so I kept them by my side. "I mean, reporting for duty."

What would she think of my intention to dig into Jones' file? I suspected she wouldn't be pleased if she caught me. I better not let her catch me then.

She nodded. "You've been assigned a supervisor, but they aren't on board currently. I urge you to familiarise yourself with the infirmary as best you can until then. Take extreme care and avoid anything you're not familiar with."

I got her message loud and clear. Look, but don't touch.

"Um, I see we have a patient already, Doctor. Perhaps I could see if they need anything."

For a moment, I thought she might refuse. Instead, she nodded and almost looked approving, and for some reason, relieved.

"Yes, do that," she said hastily. "I need to complete the inventory check."

Before I could offer to help with that, she bustled away, out the door.

"Okay then," I said under my breath. I put on my best smile and approached the cubicle. I drew the curtain aside slowly, just enough to step inside.

On the bed, a figure lay still, covered in a layer of blankets. Only his head was uncovered and that was enough to make me stare. His skin reminded me of Danec's, but with a distinctive purple hue. A Frey-taurian, I assumed. A wide bandage was wrapped around his forehead.

As I approached, he turned his face and frowned.

"Have you come to poke and prod at me too?" he asked coolly. His eyes raked me up and down, and my neat blue uniform. It was tight here and there, but it would do until I could find one that fit better.

"No," I replied cheerfully. I had met his kind a hundred times before. The type who hated to be flat on their backs, in hospital or an infirmary. Honestly, that was most people, no matter what planet they're from. Lying in a hospital bed was boring, so I didn't blame him for being grumpy. It was my job to cheer him up, if I could.

"I came to see if there's anything you need." I tugged a corner of the blanket over to straighten it.

He responded with a lazy smirk. "My cock is itchy. Care to scratch it for me?"

I raised my eyebrows at him, as if I was offended. "I'm pretty sure you can scratch it yourself."

"You can see through all of those blankets?" he asked. "I didn't know Earthians had that ability."

Earthians?

I shook my head. "We don't, I just—"

"You assumed." There was that smirk again. "Do you think you should check?"

I wasn't falling for what he wanted. He obviously thought I'd peel back the blankets and look at his— presumably—naked body. As tempting as it might be, it was also unprofessional.

Instead, I clicked on the screen beside his bed.

"It says here you fell off the railing above the engine. Hit your head, broke both... Oh. Both arms."

"Yeah, Oh." There was that smirk again. "So, about my itchy balls?"

I frowned at him over my shoulder. "I thought it was your cock that was itchy?"

He shrugged with one shoulder, then winced. "They're both itchy. I keep telling the other medics, but they ignore me. I'm thinking of filing a complaint."

I held back laughter. It wasn't nice to laugh at a patient, especially one who couldn't do things for himself. He struck me as independent, as well as arrogant.

"I suppose I could apply some lotion to stop the itch," I said. Even for a different species, a simple cream should be harmless. I had seen a bottle on a shelf near a desk, so I hurried to grab some and slipped back into the cubicle.

I snapped on a pair of gloves and started to peel back the blankets. The skin of his body was slightly lighter than his face. On the left side of his chest he sported a tattoo in the shape of a whorl. His chest and torso looked so firm I could have broken diamonds on him. Or licked him for an hour or two. Damn.

I swallowed back the thought. I had seen plenty of bodies before, enough to simply think of them clinically, as just a patient. But there was something about him…

I forced the idea away. Nursing rule number one, never get intimate with a patient.

I exposed his cock and wasn't surprised to see it was big and slightly hard. Lines of small bumps covered him from balls to tip. They protruded further when he became slightly more erect. I was tempted to touch them, to see how they felt. Professional curiosity, that was all. Or so I told myself.

"So, um, how did you fall?" I asked, determined to be all business. I poured lotion on an applicator and began to slather it over his length.

"Would you believe I was dared to stand on the railing?" he asked.

"Actually, yes," I said. "I believe it, but I have a feeling that wasn't what really happened."

I glanced at his face. His eyes were half closed. He was obviously enjoying the attention a bit too much.

"I reached for a conduit and missed," he said with a scowl. "I should have used a longer ladder, but I figured…"

"Accidents happen," I said graciously. He made a mistake and he was being punished for it. There didn't seem much point in rubbing it in. So to speak.

"Yeah." He shifted his arms and grimaced. Both were encased in bone knitters, which would heal them fully in around a week. That must seem like a long time for an active guy.

"You know, if you put on too much of that, you'll have to lick it off." He gave me a boyish smile, which I responded to with a roll of my eyes.

"And to think, I was worried you'd be different from human men," I said. "In the end, you all think with your dicks."

"Haha, ow." He sucked in a breath. "If we didn't have dicks, you women wouldn't talk to us."

I pouted at him. "That's not true. I'm talking to you, aren't I?"

"While you're creaming up my dick," he shot back.

"What's your name?" I asked.

"Slek," he replied, "son of Arron."

"I'm Edie," I said. "Has anyone told you you're incorrigible?"

"Hmmm, hot, sexy, great in bed, irresistible… No, I don't think they have."

"Consider yourself told then," I said tartly. Tentatively I touched the applicator to his balls and slathered quickly.

"Your bedside manner could use some work," he said.

"At least you won't be itchy anymore," I said.

"In a few days I'll be out of here and you'll be begging me to nail you so hard you scream," he said with such certainty I raised my eyebrows at him.

He looked back at me intently. His gaze didn't waver. He didn't even blink.

I usually didn't go for guys as self assured as him, but my mouth went dry. When he wasn't a patient, maybe, but for now…

"There, that'll do," I said quickly, my attention firmly on work. "That should keep you moist for a day or two."

He grinned. "Ah, you can play the flirting game too. I was starting to think they'd sent another dull human. There's enough of those on the *Infinity* at the best of times."

"I'm pretty sure there are dull people from every planet," I said, trying not to take offence at the dig at my home-world.

"That's true." Slek sighed. "Take Kalvix for example." He wriggled his brows. "I tried to. Take her, I mean. She wouldn't play. She's all work and no fun. You, on the other hand, seem like the kind of girl who likes to have a good time." He nodded toward his groin. "Now I'm all moist, why don't you climb on board and go for a ride?"

"I'm starting to think," I pulled the blanket back

over his cock, "that you didn't fall, but instead were pushed."

He feigned hurt. "Only if they're jealous of my prowess. Come on, I can keep a secret."

I pulled the blanket higher. "I can't begin to tell you how much trouble I would be in if I did," I said. "I'd be on the first cargo carrier back to Earth and never work as a nurse again."

"That really matters to you, doesn't it?" For a few moments at least, he was serious.

"Very much so," I said firmly.

"Would you fuck me if it wasn't against the rules?"

I frowned. "We've just met."

"That's never stopped me before," he said.

"Well, it's stopped me," I said firmly. "I like to get to know a guy first."

"Fine." He sighed loudly and shifted his rear to get more comfortable. "When I'm out of here, can I ask you out?"

"That depends, "I replied. "Are you sure no one pushed you?"

Now Slek frowned. "I'm sure, Why?"

"Because I don't want to go out with you if someone wants to hurt you. Or worse." I was only half joking.

He grinned. "I knew you'd say yes."

"You're a cocky bastard, aren't you?" I asked.

"I've been called worse," he said. "For the record, no one wants me hurt. I was a victim of my own arrogance."

"Why do I feel as though I should get that in writing?" I teased.

"Because I don't go around making admissions like that," he said. "This is a one time thing."

I shook my head. "I figured. Now, I should put this away and update your file."

"Thanks," he said. He seemed genuine.

"For what?" I asked. "I was just doing my job."

"Yeah, but my balls really *were* itchy. They were driving me crazy."

"Well, we can't have crazy patients, can we now?" I backed out of the cubicle and let the curtain fall back into place.

Speaking of crazy...

I tossed the gloves down the chute, and the applicator down another and returned the lotion to the shelf. I washed my hands thoroughly and, with several glances over my shoulder, sat at the desk.

I brought up Slek's file and Jones' and sat them side by side. If anyone came, I could hide Jones' before anyone saw.

I started there though, and read quickly. As far as I could tell, Jones had a normal childhood. The usual broken bone from falling off a hoverboard. Childhood fevers, ear infections, a cochlear implant to improve his hearing. Treatment for depression and anxiety. That had stopped a year before, after at least five years of steady treatment. The last letter from his doctor stated she had suggested more visits, but nothing in the file stood out. Nothing to suggest he was anything out of the ordinary.

I shrugged to myself and closed the file just as Kalvix walked back into the infirmary.

"How is our patient?" she asked in a tone that suggested she didn't think I'd been capable of handling him.

"He's fine, thank you, Doctor," I replied as I typed in updates. "His needs were—" I cast a sly glance toward the cubicle, "small."

"Small, my ass," Slek called out.

I chuckled.

Kalvix smiled. "You might do well here yet. He's been troubling us all over several—small issues."

"I feel ganged up on," Slek said.

I grinned. "He seems to be healing well at least. He won't be a big problem for too much longer."

"That's better." Slek sounded smug. "I can't wait to get out of here."

Kalvix smiled wryly. "No one will be happier than I will."

I wondered if he had asked her out too. It was his business, his and hers, but I couldn't help but be curious. He seemed like the kind of guy to grab every opportunity he could as often as he could. I usually avoided players, but it was only one date. How could it hurt, right?

I clicked save on his file and closed it. Thankfully Kalvix hadn't seemed to have noticed my slightly guilty look, or my distraction. I forced myself to focus, but the matter of Jones stuck in the back of my mind.

6

"I THOUGHT I might f-find you here." Danec offered me a shy smile, which I replied to with one of my own.

"I can't resist the last view of Earth before we're too far away to see it." I gestured for him to sit beside me and scooted over on the bench to make room.

"It's a bittersweet sight," he said. "I'll miss the...the ducks."

For a moment I thought I'd misheard. "Ducks?" I asked.

"Yes, ducks. They're my favourite Earth animal, apart from humans. I like their quack and the paddle of their feet under water." He mimed the action with his hands.

I smiled. "They are pretty cute. People used to eat them once." I regretted my words when his face fell. "They don't anymore," I added quickly. "At least as far as I know." I decided against telling him what humans did to chickens.

"Oh, great." He sat sideways and rested his elbow on the back of the bench. "I'm sorry about last night. I came back to look for you, but I couldn't find you. And then, well, Commander J'avet saw me and ordered me to turn in for the night." Danec looked rueful. "I don't think he likes me."

"From what I've seen of him, he doesn't like much of anyone." I swivelled to face Danec and tucked one foot behind the other. "It probably didn't help that we didn't move fast enough during the drill." I half expected to hear the alarm sound the moment the words left my lips, but it didn't.

"Yeah, I guess so." He glanced down at his lap. "Have you seen the, um, recreation centre?"

From the way he spoke, I wondered what kind of recreation he was referring to, but I decided he meant the innocent kind.

"I haven't. Is it… nice?" Really? Nice? Was that the best word I could come up with? I wanted to sink into the bench, but I smiled instead and tried to look as though I didn't feel like an idiot.

Danec nodded. If he thought anything was off, he gave no sign. "It's g-great."

I noticed he used that word a lot. He must have noticed it too, because now he looked embarrassed.

"Can I show it to you?"

If someone like Slek had asked, he would have meant something else entirely, but Danec was different. Sweeter. I didn't mind flirting, of course, but it was nice to have a friend on board. Two friends, but I hadn't seen Brinley since we boarded. I suspected her days would be spent on the bridge, or flying one of the small pods which belonged to the ship.

"I'd like that," I said.

"Great," he said. His eyes widened. "I mean good. I mean—" He stopped. "Unless you'd prefer to stay longer?" He nodded toward the window.

I exhaled through my nose. "I'll see it again some day." There wasn't much point in spending the rest of the day with my nose pressed against the glass, watching Earth become a dot in the rearview mirror, so to speak.

"I'm sure you will," he assured me, then smiled softly. "So will I."

"You're thinking of the ducks, aren't you?" I asked, half teasing.

He looked sheepish. "Yes. they remind me of the dorva bird from back home."

"Do they have paddling feet too?" I mimed the action.

"They do," he confirmed, "but they honk, rather than quack, and they have teeth." He bared his.

I grimaced. "They sound...adorable."

He chuckled. "They're mostly harmless. Unless you go too close to their burrows."

"I'll remember that if I ever visit Frey-T," I assured him. "Now, you were going to show me the rec room?"

"Right, yes," he said quickly. He rose and stepped away from the bench to let me out. "I'm sorry, I can't pull the chair out this time."

I laughed, because as far as I could tell, every bit of furniture was bolted to the deck.

"Not without getting into trouble anyway. You don't want to get thrown out the airlock."

He looked confused for a moment. "Oh, that's a reference to Earth science fiction movies, right?"

"Right," I said. "I've seen, like, every one ever made. Even the bad ones."

Danec frowned. "Why would anyone make a bad movie?"

I snorted. "That's a very good question. I don't

know why. I guess they didn't realise it was bad at the time."

"Oh, I see. I suppose it's a matter of opinion as well."

"That too." I followed him to the ship's elevator bank.

He pressed the 'up' button and we waited. After a minute or two, one of the doors slid open silently and we stepped inside.

"It's on level five." He pressed the second button from the top.

I knew there was a level above that as well, which was only accessible from a secure part of level six. What was up there, I could only guess. I considered asking Danec, but I doubted anyone would tell a lowly ensign, any more than they'd tell a lowly nurse. I wondered if Slek knew. As an engineer, he should have intimate knowledge of every part of the ship. I made a mental note to ask him the next time I saw him.

The elevator door slid open to a corridor. On one side were several closed doors. On the other, was a single open one. From that doorway came the sounds of laughter and something that might be a computer game.

I stepped into the doorway to see a room full of

long couches, tables and chairs and a wide screen on the opposite wall.

In front of that stood several people, a human or two, a woman from Frey-T, two from Agus and a yellow skinned Centauri man. They all had controllers in their hands and were moving avatars inside some kind of game. As far as I could work out, they were exploring a damaged spaceship and shooting androids whenever one appeared.

Space Invaders, present day version. It was certainly more advanced than anything I had played. The ship on the screen looked real enough to put my hand in and touch it.

"There's a library room in the back," Danec said. "It's quieter there than in here. The computer bank holds copies of almost every book ever published."

"I hope the authors get royalties," I remarked.

"Of course. The IF believes in fostering the arts," Danec said.

I nodded and scanned the room. "Is that a chess set?"

"Yes, do you play?"

"No, I've just never seen one that wasn't on a screen." I walked over and picked up a pawn. It was carved from wood, with a base covered in a circle of black felt. Such craftsmanship hadn't been seen on Earth for a couple of generations. I certainly hadn't expected to see it here.

"Chess is a game of subtlety. It takes an intelligent mind to grasp it properly."

I knew that voice before I turned around to see the disapproving look on J'avet's face. He stood with another Parvoran who had the same disdain on his features.

"Is that so?" I tossed the pawn into the air and caught it on my palm. "Seems like just a game to me."

J'avet looked as if he wanted to snatch the piece out of my hand. "I wouldn't expect you to understand."

"Interesting." I tossed the piece again. "Because you know nothing about me."

This time he grabbed the pawn out of the air and put it back in place on the board. "I know your kind. Flighty, thoughtless, disrespectful."

"Sir—" Danec started.

He was silenced with a look from J'avet.

"You would do better to stay away from her, ensign," J'avet said coldly.

"Sir, I—"

"We're friends." I managed a good bit of frost in

my tone as well. "Do you actually have the authority to make those kinds of decisions for him?"

J'avet stepped closer to me, until his nose was a handspan from mine. "I have the authority to have you put you on night shifts, and him on days until we reach Agus. I have the authority to order you both to refrain from fraternising. I have the authority to throw you both in the brig."

I swallowed. Not because I was scared of him, but because his proximity threatened to set my blood on fire.

"Commander," Danec began.

I interrupted him. "We're doing nothing wrong," I said coldly. After all, it was him who had approached us and insulted my intelligence, literally. I was furious, but I managed to contain myself, at least for now.

"See you don't," J'avet said. "One toe out of line and you will be in the brig until we reach Agus. Upon our arrival there, you'll be placed on the first ship back to Earth."

I had never wanted to punch someone more than I wanted to punch him. If I didn't believe his threat, I might have. Unfortunately I did believe it. I would have to watch myself, especially when he was around.

"We'll both be... be model passengers, sir," Danec stammered.

"See you are," J'avet said without taking his eyes off me. "I'd hate it if you shared her fate because of your poor taste in...friends." He glanced toward Danec and nodded.

"I'm sure both of you have somewhere else to be." Apparently he wasn't going to order us to avoid each other, at least not yet.

"Yes, Commander." I actually managed to keep sarcasm out of my voice. Gold star for me.

"Yes, sir." Danec put a hand on my shoulder and steered me toward the door.

It wasn't until the elevator doors closed that I let my anger show.

"Who does he think he is?" I snapped. "Surely the rec room is there for everyone?"

Danec sighed. "It is. I think I angered him when I didn't respond to the drill fast enough. He thinks I'm incompetent." He looked so sad, my heart went out to him.

I put an arm around him and gave him a hug.

He looked at me in surprise and his eyes lingered on mine for a moment. He swallowed audibly, then looked down at his feet.

"I don't think it's you," I assured him. "It's me he

doesn't like." I had no idea what I had done, but his attitude pissed me off. At least let me screw up before you decide you don't like me. Then it might be justified.

"They said Parvorians are difficult," Danec said.

"They were right." I tucked a curl behind my ear, then did it again after it popped straight out. "From now on, I'll do my best to avoid him."

"Good idea," Danec said. "Is he what you humans would call an asshole or a dickhead? Or a prick?"

I laughed. Leave it to Danec to turn this into a learning experience. "I'd say he's all three. And a few more words as well."

Danec nodded. "Asshole-dickhead-prick. That's quite a mouthful."

"I recommend you don't call him that to his face," I said. Although I would dearly love to.

Danec laughed, but cut it off when the doors slid open. "We shouldn't allow ourselves to be over-heard," he said softly.

"Right." We would have to watch our backs until we reached Agus. I wasn't going to let any asshole-dickhead-prick get the better of me. No way. What-ever his problem was, it was his problem, not mine. He could carry around his groundless grudge, if that's what made him happy. I would forget all about him and get on with my life and my work.

If only I could forget how it felt to be that close to him. Perhaps a nice cold shower would help. Or a workout session with my trusty vibrator. We couldn't get to Agus soon enough, as far as I was concerned.

7

I'M sure it's a complete coincidence that I had night shifts every night for the next week. Kalvix and the other medics kept me so busy I had no time for more than a few words with Slek. I stumbled into my cabin just as Brinley was heading out for her shift. I would mutter tired words and she'd respond with sleepy ones. At least I didn't see J'avet, but I didn't see Danec either.

"Our patient's bone knitters come off today," Kalvix said as she walked into the infirmary right at seven am. "I trust you'll have no problem staying on for a while longer."

I suppressed a groan. "Yes, Doctor, of course." Truthfully, the night shift had been a long one.

A human woman had cut her finger and needed a couple of stitches.

A man from Garvi-3 had a kink in his tentacles, which I didn't know how to deal with. The doctor on duty had connected him to a machine that seemed to administer some kind of electric shock. The man had jerked, and his tentacles shot out like an angry puffer fish.

For a moment I thought he was in pain, but he smiled.

"That was exactly what I needed, thanks doc." He gave me a nod and made his way out the door.

"That was interesting," I remarked.

The doctor smiled. "Garvians are interesting folk." He was an older man, who spoke with a low, warm rumble. "They're technically blind, as we understand vision, but they use electric impulses to guide them around. When they've overdone it, they need a brief recharge."

"So their tentacles flop when they're tired?" I said.

The doctor chuckled. "In a manner of speaking, yes. Ordinarily they'd plug themselves in while they sleep, but sometimes that's not enough."

"That's cool," I said. Strange, but cool.

"Very." The doctor nodded and went back to his desk.

I went back to mine and opened the file on Garvi-3 so I could read more. With Slek asleep, and every surface spotlessly clean, there was little else for me to do. No nurse wished for a busy shift, but this was slower than I preferred. By the time it was over, I was ready to eat and sleep.

Until Kalvix arrived.

I followed her to Slek's bed and slipped in behind the curtain.

The purple guy from Frey-T was already awake and waiting for us. He'd managed to work himself up so he was sitting, but his arms stuck out uncomfortably.

"Oh good, you're both here." He grinned. "Time for a sponge bath and maybe a quick blow job?"

"It's time to remove those." Kalvix nodded toward the bone knitter closest to her. "You'll be able to wash and pleasure yourself soon enough."

Slek pouted. "But it's so much more fun when someone else does it. Wouldn't you agree, Edie?" He quirked an eyebrow at me.

"Sure," I said with a shrug, "but it's time you scratched your own itches."

From the deadpan look on Kalvix's face, she had read the file.

"She's spent too much time with you," Slek told

the doctor. "She's become a spoilsport already." He raised a finger at me. "Don't forget we have a date planned after I get out of here. That," he paused for emphasis, "is imminent."

Kalvix shot me a look.

I suppose, unlike J'avet, she didn't care who her subordinates fraternised with outside their work hours. Maybe she thought I had dubious taste. Either way, she said nothing.

"I haven't forgotten," I assured Slek.

"Have you removed bone knitters before?" Kalvix asked.

"Yes, Doctor." I nodded.

"Very well." She waved at me to take off the left one, while she unwound the bandage from Slek's head.

He winced at her, then at me while I undid the clasps which held the knitters shut. Carefully, because the newly healed bone was still tender, I worked the knitter apart as wide as the hinges would allow.

"Can you lift your arm?" I asked.

Gingerly, Slek raised his arm so I could slide the knitter out from underneath it.

"It feels so light now," he said.

"Of course it does," I replied. "And look how puny

your arm is." It was anything but. He was all muscle from his shoulder to the tips of his long, thick fingers.

He grinned and laughed. "You're a hard woman, Nurse Wright." He winced as Kalvix eased the gauze from his head wound. "Not as hard as you though, Doctor."

"Keep still," Kalvix said.

I didn't blame him for wincing. His head was a mess of fading bruises and a healing gash that must have hurt like a bitch.

I slipped out between the curtains to grab an X-ray wand and came back as Kalvix was applying some kind of blue substance to Slek's wound.

I passed the X-ray wand over Slek's arm and watched the small screen.

"I'm seeing a newly healed bone," I said. "It looks straight."

Kalvix nodded. As the doctor, she would double check, but I was confident she'd agree.

"Remove the other knitter, please," she instructed.

I stepped around to the other side of the bed and did as she asked.

"Another puny arm," I teased. What did he do for exercise, lift shuttles? I didn't ask him that, though.

He seemed to have a healthy enough ego as it was. Besides, I knew my expression spoke volumes.

"This bone looks good too," I said.

"All my bones are impressive," Slek said with a sly smile. "Especially my cock."

"A penis is not a bone," I said dryly.

"Not right now it's not," he agreed, "but with a little encouragement— Ouch!"

"Sorry." Kalvix didn't sound sorry. "We can heal bones, but bruises need time. Perhaps don't land on your head."

"Thanks, I'll remember that next time I fall," Slek said sarcastically.

"Make sure you do." Kalvix took the X-ray wand when I offered it to her and waved it over his arms. "You're fit to leave, but I need to see you every morning to have that head wound assessed."

"Yes ma'am." He gave her a cheeky salute and swung his legs off the bed. The blankets fell aside, revealing his still naked body, ridiculous muscles and all.

"Nurse, bring him some clothes, please," Kalvix said. She averted her eyes, I suspected out of respect for her patient rather than because his nudity made her uncomfortable. She was too professional to behave otherwise. She stepped out of the cubicle with a shake of her head.

"No need, I'm not modest," Slek stood fully upright. He stood over a head taller than me.

"You might not be," I said, "but the rest of the ship doesn't need to be subjected to your—"

"Puny muscles?" he finished with a smirk.

"Exactly," I said. "There's no cure for that kind of trauma."

He chuckled. "So, about that date. Should we go now, or can I bend you over the bed and pound you silly?"

"If you harass my staff, I'll have to report you to your superior officer," Kalvix said from outside the curtain.

"*Now* you object," Slek said, loud enough for her to hear. "I think she likes me, deep down."

A snort and the sound of footsteps moving away was the only response his comment got.

"Wait there, I'll see what I can find." I slipped out without a glance over my shoulder and headed for the wardrobe where spare clothes were kept for times like this. I found a shirt and a pair of trousers in IF grey which should fit well enough, and took them back in. I handed them both to him and stood back while he dressed.

"I was serious about the date," he said. He winced a little while he pulled the shirt over his shoulders. "I know just the place."

"I'm sure you do, but it's breakfast time and I probably look a mess." I didn't need to consult a mirror to know much of my hair had exploded out of my hair-tie and sat around my head like a crown of fuzz.

"You look beautiful," he said firmly. "I don't offer to nail every girl I see, you know."

"Mmmhmm," I said, disbelieving.

"It's true," he protested. "Just the cute ones."

I might have stood up a bit taller. "You think I'm cute?"

"You're adorable," he said. "You must have guys chasing you right and left."

"Not exactly, no," I replied. "Some even hate my guts." I debated telling him about J'avet, but it didn't seem fair to get him involved in the situation, especially if he had to work with the man.

"Their loss." He buttoned up his shirt and leaned against the bed to pull on his pants.

"That's true," I agreed. Unless the asshole-dick-head-prick made Danec's life more difficult.

"What about tonight?" Slek zipped up his fly, after making a show of trying to tuck his cock in, as if it might be too big to fit. Maybe it was. "I can't work for a few more days, so I know I'm free."

"I'm on two days off after this," I replied.

He grinned. "Perfect, we can have dinner and then spend the next two days in bed."

"You're very sure I'll sleep with you," I said.

"I'm an eternal optimist," he said unapologetically. His expression turned serious for a moment. "I'm also a shameless flirt, in case you hadn't guessed, but I will respect you if you say no. Although, you've seen my dick, who wouldn't want to—"

"Engineer Slek," Kalvix's warning tone came from just outside the curtain.

"Oops, she's using my job title. She must be really pissed," Slek said loudly.

"Can you blame her?" I teased.

While he pretended to be hurt, Kalvix didn't bother to suppress a bark of laughter.

"See, she does like me," Slek said. He stuck his head out the curtain, then tugged it aside on the rail.

"Interesting theory," Kalvix said from the sink where she stood, washing her hands. Her antennas turned toward us, as if keeping an extra set of eyes on him.

Slek scratched his forehead. "So, no threesome then?"

"If you don't leave, I'll call security," Kalvix said, but she didn't look too serious. Yet.

"All right, all right, I'm going." He held his hands out to either side.

"Me too," I said. "Unless you need me for anything further?"

Kalvix waved me out the door with the cloth she used to dry her hands. "Enjoy your days off."

"I will. Thank you, Doctor." I could have skipped, but I walked out the door, weary and hungry. To Slek I said, "I'm in room seventy-seven. I'll see you at seven."

He saluted with a smile. "I'll be right on time." He turned smartly on a heel and winced as his bare foot squeaked on the floor. "That would have worked much better with boots on," he said over his shoulder.

I chuckled and started toward my room. Before I took a handful of steps, I spotted Jones, hands holding something to his chest. His eyes shifted this way and that, as though he was searching for some-one, or hoping not to be seen. A Centaurian passed him and he looked down at the floor until he was past.

He drew himself up and strode down the corridor, but my suspicion was already piqued. He was up to something and I wanted to know what. I should probably call security and let them deal with it, but they might only scare him away. For whatever reason, he seemed to think he could talk to me. He might do that now, but I didn't want to confront him directly.

I changed direction and followed him at a distance

Jones ducked around a corner and into another section of the corridor. I stopped at a discreet distance and waited, but he didn't come back out. A sign on the wall next to the corridor was in English and a few other alien languages. It read, 'Communications and navigation.'

Nothing suspicious about him going in there. Maybe.

I hurried across and peered down into the corridor. A woman from Agus stepped out of a doorway and gave me a funny look.

Now who seemed suspicious?

I flashed her a smile. "I think this is the right place. This ship is a maze, don't you think?"

"Uh, indeed." She hurried away without a backwards glance.

I made a face to myself and moved carefully in the direction Jones had gone.

The room the woman had stepped out of was wall to wall vidscreens and about half a dozen occupants from different planets. All calling home, I presumed. I would have to do the same at some point, but until now I'd been too busy to give it much thought. My mother would be wondering how I was doing. My siblings too, if they took a moment from their busy lives to think about me.

Yeah, none of us would win the prize for keeping in touch.

I straightened my back and marched past the doorway as though I belonged in that part of the ship, and kept walking. If that was communications, then navigation must be—

"Why are you following me?" Jones hissed.

He appeared in front of me so suddenly it took a moment to register.

"Where did you come from?" I asked. "What makes you think I'm following you?" I crossed my arms over my chest and tried to stare him down. He was only the same age as me, maybe even a little younger, but his eyes were blue chips of bitterness and ice.

"Navigation," he said icily. "I wanted to see how long until we reach Agus."

I narrowed my eyes. "You know as well as I do

how long the journey is." I noticed then that whatever he'd held to his chest, he no longer had it. His arms hung by his sides, hands curled half into fists. "What are you really doing here?"

"I could ask you the same thing," he said, "if you weren't following me."

I exhaled in frustration. "Fine, I was following you, but only because you looked suspicious."

He frowned, then shrugged. "If I did, it's because I don't trust *anyone* on board."

I didn't miss the emphasis. "I thought humans were okay, as far as you were concerned?"

"Until they start following me," he retorted.

"Touché. You still haven't said why you're really here."

"Like I said, I wanted to know—"

I interrupted. "I don't buy it."

He growled in the back of his throat. "I get caught up in studying. I lose track of time. I thought it was the third day of the week, but it's the fourth. I assumed my watch was faulty." He held up his wrist. Around it, he wore a watch the same as mine.

"That's what you were holding?" I asked.

He looked confused for a moment, then nodded. "I was ready to throw it at a wall if it was that off. Turns out, it was me who was off." He gave an awkward laugh, but there was something in his eyes that suggested he wasn't telling the whole story, and that he wouldn't, even if I pushed.

I considered my next words, and went with a gentle tease, in the hope it might defuse the situation somewhat.

"That's really dorky. Maybe you should take a break once in a while."

He snorted. "Yeah, that's what my father used to say before he worked himself to death."

"Oh." So much for making things better. "I'm sorry. That must have been difficult."

He rubbed the bridge of his nose with one finger. "I guess. I hardly saw him, so it's no great loss, I guess."

"I don't know, it hurts to lose someone you love." I spoke from experience, but only older, frail and not well known aunts and uncles. It still stung each time.

"Yeah, I guess. Do you want to get a coffee?" His expression was so guarded, I couldn't tell if he hoped I'd say no or yes.

"I really can't," I said regretfully. "It's been a long shift and I need to grab a sandwich and some sleep."

He seemed indifferent to my response, but at least he didn't get angry again.

"Fine. Another time maybe."

"Sure. I need a coffee quite often. If I see you in the mess, I'll say hi. Or, you know, if I see you skulking around the corridors."

Anger flashed in his eyes for a moment. "I wasn't —" He must have realised I was teasing because he stopped and sucked in a breath. "You're joking. Sorry, sometimes I just…"

"It's okay." I put a hand lightly on his shoulder, but drew it back when he frowned at it. "If you ever need to talk, I'm here for you. Or one of the doctors."

"I don't need their help," he snapped. He rubbed the bridge of his nose again. "I should go."

"Yeah." I stepped back away from him and let him stalk past me, back down the corridor. "I'll see you later."

"Yeah," he said over his shoulder. "Later."

He disappeared around the corner and was gone.

It wasn't until I turned back in the direction of my room that I realised his file hadn't said anything about his father dying.

8

"ARE you sure we're allowed up here?" I gripped the railing in both hands and peered over the edge into the near darkness. The only light below came from a bank of controls on the far side of the lower level, near a door.

"Of course we're not," Slek said. He turned the light on his watch. "That's half the fun." He must have seen my expression because he grinned, white teeth flashing in the dark.

"Don't worry, we won't get caught. No one comes here, especially at night. Except to do maintenance, and no one's rostered for that right now. I checked."

"If you're wrong, you'll be in the brig right beside me," I said in a playful growl. I assumed they wouldn't send an engineer back to his home world in disgrace, but he could still get in a lot of trouble.

"I'll happily share a cell with you," he said, his smile lopsided. "Imagine the things we could get up to in there."

"Nothing, they'd have security watching us all the time," I said dryly.

He made a dismissive sound. "A minor inconvenience. Besides, I would soon make you forget all about them." His hand brushed across my ass and I jumped.

He chuckled. "Come on, I have everything set up over here."

'Everything' consisted of a blanket spread out on the floor near the wall, and a picnic basket, made of metal. Okay, it was a maintenance bucket, but I appreciated the look he was going for.

He knelt on the blanket and switched on a small light which sat to one side.

The light flashed frantically, like an emergency light.

I held up my hand in front of my eyes and squinted against the sudden, pulsating glare.

"Oops, wrong setting." He flicked a switch on the side and the light settled to a single, soft glow.

I lowered my hand and took in the sight of him

on his knees on the blanket. He wore casual clothes. Black trousers and a black shirt which was so tight around his enormous biceps that I didn't know how the seams held together. On his feet he wore boots which looked well worn. Also black.

In comparison, my aqua t-shirt and black pants looked like a riot of colour.

"This is romantic," I said. Honestly, I was surprised. I wasn't used to guys doing sweet things like this. Usually it was a fast food meal and an action movie. Both awesome things, but not very intimate. Perhaps I had misjudged his flirty nature. There was clearly more to him than I had suspected. I reminded myself to keep an open mind from now on.

I sat on the blanket with my back to the wall. My hand tingled from where it touched his. It was a different feeling to Danec's touch, but just as heady. The butterflies in my stomach moved around in lazy spirals.

"We're not allowed alcohol on board, so we have water or synth milk." Slek reached into the bucket and pulled out a bottle of each.

"Water is fine, thank you." I accepted the metal cup, full to the brim when he handed it to me and quickly sipped to keep from spilling it. "Delicious."

Recycled umpteen times, it didn't exactly taste fresh, but it was drinkable.

"I looked for champagne glasses, but for some reason the *Infinity* doesn't have any." He made a face. "Something about wasting space and not being a priority. Blah, blah. Anyway, we also have sandwiches." He drew out a plate. "Vegetables, garu nut butter, synthcheese, or honey?"

"Honey?" I echoed, unable to keep the excitement from my voice. "Is it real?"

Slek tried to look insulted, but he ruined it with his smile. "Yes, a friend brought a few jars from Earth. I managed to score a couple." He handed me a honey sandwich on brown bread.

"By score do you mean your friend doesn't know you have them?" I asked. A smile tugged at the corners of my mouth. Being around him made it hard not to smile and laugh. He was fun to be around. What was the old saying? Never a dull moment.

Slek laughed. "No, he knows. I might have over exaggerated the amount of pain my injuries caused, so he'd take pity, but it was voluntary on his part."

"More or less," I said.

"Well, yes," he agreed, without a hint of shame or regret. "I owe him now though."

I bit into my sandwich and savoured the sweetness of genuine, sticky honey. It tasted like home and deliciousness.

"Mmmm, totally worth it. So, do you come here often?" *Geez, Edie, why don't you say the corniest line in the book?* I mentally cringed at myself.

"All the time," he replied around a mouthful. "I fell over the railing right beside you."

"Ah." I glanced at it as though it might give way at any moment. "That's very... romantic." It was certainly an interesting location for a date.

"Isn't it though?" he agreed. "Scene of the crime and all."

"I thought you fell?"

"Scene of the accident, then. Actually," he looked serious for a moment, "I was nervous about coming up here. I thought if I had a good memory, it might help me when I have to get back to work. Is that weird?" The side of his mouth drew back as if he expected me to laugh.

"It's sweet," I told him. "I'm glad I could help in some way."

He blinked in surprise, then fist pumped the air. "I've never been called sweet before."

I laughed. "Don't let it go to your head too much."

"Which head?" he shot back immediately.

"Either," I replied firmly. Silence fell for a moment before I said, "Can I ask you a question?"

"Anything," he said. "If you're going to ask if you can suck my cock, the answer is yes."

"I wasn't," I replied. I ignored his pout and said, "I know a guy, a friend, who is also from Frey-T. He seems a lot more, uh, innocent than you. His knowledge of humans comes from a vidscreen."

"Mine comes from being on the *Infinity* for a few years," Slek replied easily. "And fucking a number of them."

"I see." I should have known what his response would be. "You've been with a few of us?"

"Well…" He drew out the word.

"One or two?" I cocked my head.

"Um…"

"Slek?" I raised my eyebrows.

"What? Zero is a number," he said sheepishly. "I have interacted with a lot of humans and tried to sleep with the pretty ones, okay?"

I shrugged. "Okay, but why not be honest about it?"

"I have a reputation to uphold. What would people think?"

"I don't know, does it really matter what they think?" I creased my brow and watched him intently.

He hesitated. "I guess not." He paused again before he added, "I care what you think."

"Because you want to sleep with me?" I finished my last bite of sandwich and washed it down.

"No," he said firmly. "I mean yes, I do, but I care what you think because I like you. Most humans are kinda dull and..." he grinned, "puny. But you're cute and funny and smart. And—"

"Yes?" Did I really want to know what he had to add?

"No one on Frey-T, or most of the planets I know, have curly hair. It's..." He cocked his head. "It's special."

I put a hand to my hair and blushed furiously. "You think so?"

"I *know* so," he said. "What a fascinating shade of pink your skin has become. Are you part Parvoran, by any chance? Wait, no, you don't seem furry enough. Not in any places I've seen yet, anyway."

I blushed harder. "I'm one hundred percent human," I muttered. "And not furry, except where I'm meant to have fur. I mean my eyebrows," I added quickly.

"Of course you did." He laughed. "So, why don't you tell me more about yourself."

"What do you want to know?" I asked. I hoped the blush would fade quickly.

"Everything." He reclined on his elbow and toasted me with a cup of synthmilk. "Start with where you were born."

He listened intently while I told him about my childhood, my parents, my tendency to nurse my siblings while they were sick, which led me to go into the profession. I told him why I left Earth and how much I loved chocolate.

"I'll have to remember that," he said. "I think I'm going to have to work hard if I'm going to impress you."

"Yes, you do," I said, only half joking. "What about you?"

"What about me?" He leaned back against the wall, a lazy smile on his lips. "I'm already impressed with myself."

I swatted him on the arm. When I touched his skin, my fingers burned like I'd swiped my hand across a hot stove. More electricity than the jolt the Garvian had received, shot through me, to the last drop of blood which now pounded in every vein like a hammer.

Slek's lips dropped apart and I knew he felt it too. It was more than desire. It was a yearning to be close to him, to find out everything. To understand the man behind the flirtation. Okay, it was desire as well, I'm only human.

"I told you everything about myself," I said softly. "Now I want to know about you."

"I have a feeling," he said, his voice the same pitch, "that I've only started to scratch the surface." He sucked in a breath and his usual boyishness was back. "I was born in the capital of Frey-T. My father was a teacher, my mother is an engineer. She designs ships like this." He gestured around the room with his cup. "So guys like me can complain about the bad design when we have to repair things. Before you ask, no, she never listens to my suggestions. If she had, there would be Blarviun ale running through the pipes instead of water."

"I don't fancy the idea of showering in ale." I wrinkled my nose.

"That's what she said. In your case, I would happily lick it all off." He stuck out his tongue and licked the air a couple of times. The end split in two, like a snake's.

A shiver passed through me. I could imagine him doing a few things with that tongue…

I cleared my throat, but it did little to suppress the throb in my body.

"That wouldn't work for everyone on board," I said, my voice higher than usual. "Commander J'avet, for one." I meant it as a joke, but the image of the Parvoran sucking ale off my breasts popped into my head. Just the thought made me wet as hell. Okay, more wet.

"It might do him some good," Slek said. "He might lighten up a little."

"Yeah." I really needed to change the subject before I made a total mess of my panties. "So you went into engineering because your mother did it, or just to get ale into the pipes?"

He chuckled. "I had an aptitude for it. My father was disappointed." His expression turned rueful. "Teaching is a traditionally male job on Frey-T. He wanted me to follow him. Can you imagine me teaching university?"

"I can imagine you getting into trouble with every pretty student who came your way," I replied.

"Yeah, I probably wouldn't have lasted very long. It's safer to work with machines. They don't mind if you get intimate with them." A frown crossed his features. "I don't mean like *that*. That would be weird. I mean you touch them and they don't complain. Unless they're androids. Some of those really hate being repaired. I met one once who swore it tickled every time I tried to unscrew a bolt." He shook his head and furrowed his brow, but looked amused.

"Is that even possible?" I asked. My knowledge of androids and robots was limited to the ones in factories, which put together vehicles and technology. I'd never actually seen one.

"Yes and no," he replied. "Technically, machines can't feel anything, but their creators can make them think they can. I'm not sure if they want to make them like living beings, or if they're just smart asses."

"Both?" I suggested.

He scratched his forehead. "Possibly. Personally, I don't see the point. Imagine if the *Infinity* was more alive. She might throw us off if we touch her the wrong way."

"Perhaps that was what happened." I waved at the healing wound on his head.

"Now you mention it, that makes sense." He looked thoughtful. "I should be more careful how I handle the old girl from now on."

I shook my head at him and smiled. I couldn't picture him being rough with the ship. After all, if he broke it, he'd have to fix it.

"Siblings?" I asked.

"Two sisters, both older," he replied. "They liked to play with me like I was a doll."

"I can see you in a dress and a pretty pink wig," I teased.

He put his empty cup in the bucket and took mine from my fingers when I nodded that I was done.

"The funny thing is, that's exactly what I would put myself in." He leaned back against the wall again and cupped his hands behind his head. "A curly pink wig and yellow dress stuffed full so I had big boobs." He wiggled his eyebrows at me and grinned.

"I'm sure you were very pretty," I said, trying not to laugh. He would have looked adorable and I had no issue with people of any gender or species dressing however they liked.

"The prettiest," he agreed. "But not as pretty as you." He leaned in to catch a curl around his finger. He twirled it slowly and stared in fascination as though he'd never touched hair before. "You're so soft." His voice broke on the last word. "I had no idea."

I blushed.

He smiled and moved his hand to the back of my head, feather light, stroking in wonder. He caught up a handful and gently pulled me to him.

My eyes locked on his. I had never seen that shade of blue before. They looked as if they should crackle with electricity.

"Edie." His breath brushed my cheek, warm and scented with honey. Sweet and hot, all at the same time.

"Mmmhmm?" I couldn't be trusted with actual words right now.

"Can I kiss you?"

"Mmmhmm." My eyes half closed, stomach fluttered with nervous anticipation.

When his lips met mine, I wanted to explode and implode all at once. Fire danced through my veins like flames on tinder dry wood.

He kissed me gently, softy, barely more than a brush before he pulled away.

"I want so much more," he said, his voice husky, "but I don't want to spoil this. I don't want to rush."

I nodded. Part of me wanted him to pin me beneath him and pound me until I screamed, but I wanted more with him than just sex.

"Agreed," I said reluctantly. "No rushing. We have —" I was going to say, 'all the time in the world' but in truth, we had this journey. Once we reached Agus, I would get off the *Infinity* and he wouldn't. My heart sank a little, but if there was anything to this, we would make it work.

"I—"

His words were interrupted by an enormous bang and the deck shifted under us.

9

"WHAT THE—" The deck slanted and I was thrown painfully against the rail. Tears of pain sprang to my eyes. I blinked and cleared them as the bucket and lights slid through a gap and were gone.

We were plunged into darkness.

Slek said something which sounded like, "Not again," and grunted. He reached for my hands and pulled me to him. His arms went around me and he held me while the ship canted the other way.

"Fuck." I gasped as we hit the wall, although he shielded me from the worst of the impact. "Your bones are still—"

"I'm fine. We need to get out of here."

An alarm sounded once, twice. A voice thundered out speakers a metre or two overhead.

"All personnel and passengers, make your way to the pod bay, immediately. This is not a drill. I repeat, make your way to the pod bay and prepare to evacuate the ship. This is *not* a drill."

"Getting out of here is a good idea," I said. Blood slammed through my ears, which rang from the volume of the warning. The silence which followed was almost as loud.

"Yeah." Slek grabbed my hand and pulled me to my feet.

I turned the light on my watch and he did the same with his.

"Don't let go," he said.

He didn't need to tell me twice. Truthfully I wasn't sure I could release my grip on him if I wanted to. The warmth of his skin helped keep my fear at bay.

He tugged me back toward the hatch which led out of the engine room. Thank goodness we didn't have to climb a ladder to get down, although the hatch was small. Designed only for maintenance and not regular traffic, we both had to duck while we stepped over the threshold. My heart hammered all the way, sure that with one more cant in the wrong direction, we'd be flung off the railing and into the engine.

We stepped out of the hatch and into the chaos of confused passengers and ship personnel.

"It must be bad if they aren't calling for you to fix it," I said, breathless with fear and adrenaline.

"All the more reason we should hurry." He pulled me between two dazed looking Centaurians, who seemed to have been woken from a deep sleep by the alarm.

"Brinley," I said quickly. "And Danec. What if they're asleep?" I couldn't leave them.

The alarm sounded again, even louder out here than in the engine room.

I winced at the noise. "On second thought, I doubt they would sleep through that." Still, I scanned the corridor ahead for a sign of either of them.

"Slek," I said after a few moments.

"Yes, Edie?"

My tongue darted over my lips. "Please tell me there's enough pods for everyone."

The woman in front of me turned and gave me a horrified look before she hurried on.

"More than enough," Slek assured me. "Frey-T learnt that lesson after the first ship needed to be evacuated."

"Was it called Titanic?" I asked ironically.

He gave me a funny look. "No. *Dreevam*, after our first president."

"Ah. Ow." A man from Agus stepped on my toe in his attempt to push past us. "We'll all get there."

No sooner had I said that than the ship rocked again. We were thrown against each other, and the wall.

Someone screamed and I realised it was me.

Slek's hand gripped mine tighter than ever. "We need to reach the end of this corridor, then—"

"Then what?" I asked, my voice high.

"We take an elevator or service shaft."

"If the power goes out while we're on an elevator—"

"We're fucked," he finished for me. "Service shaft it is." He pulled me so hard I almost had to run to keep up. We skidded to a stop at the end of the line which led to a hole in the wall. A security officer with the tentacles of a Garvian directed people one by one into a dark hole in the side of the wall.

"One at a time in an orderly manner," he said calmly. "One at a time."

In spite of that, the crowd pushed and jostled as people pressed to reach the chute first.

Someone else stepped on my foot, but at this point I was too scared to growl at them.

Slek squeezed my hand. "It's okay. We'll be fine."

The ship rocked and I squealed. "Are you sure?" Right now, I didn't feel very certain. Anything but.

"I'm absolutely sure. Look, we're next." He nodded toward the chute. How he or the Garvian could be so calm, I didn't know, but I drew on my training for emergencies and forced myself to breathe.

The voice over the loudspeaker repeated the warning to evacuate the ship.

"We're trying to," I muttered. Then I was face to face with the deep, dark hole. And the chute which disappeared around a bend and out of sight.

"Ladies first." Slek said. "It's just a big slide. It's usually used for dirty laundry."

"Wonderful," I muttered. "For the record, that isn't the kind of dirty talk I like." I let him help me through the hole, so I was sitting at the top of the chute.

He chuckled. "You have your watch and I'm right on your ass," he said. "I'll be thinking dirty thoughts all the way down."

All the innuendos and no time to enjoy them.

I sucked in a breath and might have hesitated, but he gave me a shove and I started to slide. With nothing to hold on to and no way to slow myself, I gritted my teeth and tried not to scream. I felt as though I was in free-fall, with no net and no end, just round and round in a loop, faster and faster.

I let out a whimper which bubbled up in my chest. It bubbled harder and harder until I wasn't sure I could stop myself from screaming and screaming.

Just before I did, I slid out the end of the long tube and into the arms of someone who thrust me aside the moment I regained my feet. They turned to do the same for Slek, but he flew out of the chute with a grin and landed like a cat.

"You've done that before," I said.

"A time or two." He reclaimed my hand and we made our way with the throng toward the rear of the ship. A lot of people were dressed in IF regulation pyjamas, but some were naked. I guess when a disembodied voice tells you to leave immediately, you do just that.

I thought I caught a glimpse of Kalvix, but she was swept away before I could be sure.

The push and jostle resumed at the entrance to the pod bay, which was wide enough for four or five people, but not the eight or nine which were trying to get through all at once.

Slek and I stopped and waited along with the rest, taking only small steps every few moments.

I was so focused on the doorway I didn't see anyone approach until I was almost knocked off my feet.

"Edie!" Brinley almost shouted in my ear. She hugged me so hard I could barely breathe. "You're all right!"

"Yes." I drew my head away from her and winced. "You too. Do you know what happened?"

Brinley shook her head. "Something about an explosion in or near the navigation array. They're worried whatever caused it will spread."

The ship rocked again and a bang sounded, followed by another.

"Shit," I muttered.

"Yes, come on." Brinley grabbed my spare hand and pulled. "I've been assigned to pod twelve. I was on my way there when I saw you." She blinked at Slek, who was still attached to my other hand. "You can come too."

"Thanks," he said dryly, but let himself be pulled through the crowds to the doorway.

"Pilot coming through," Brinley said, her voice brisk, businesslike.

The crowd muttered, but they parted to let us

pass. I ignored the glares. They would all get on a pod, but without a pilot, they wouldn't leave. Without a nurse, their injuries would go untreated. I made every justification I could think of, but I still felt guilty for pushing in.

I forgot about it a moment later when Danec, with a worried look on his face, spotted me. His face split in a broad smile. My heart promptly flipped, because it has no idea about appropriate timing.

"You're okay," he said happily.

"Have you been assigned a pod?" Brinley asked. When he shook his head, she nodded. "You're with us then, ensign." She nodded up ahead. "Pod twelve. It will be up to you to make sure we have no more than fifty on board. That's more than I'd like and we'll have to recycle the oxygen more quickly, but any less and we won't all get off this ship."

"Yes, ma'am," Danec said. "I can do that." He drew himself up taller and made his face look stern. He looked a bit like he needed to pee, but when it came down to it, he would do as she asked. All of our lives depended on it.

We pushed through to our pod and Brinley keyed in a code on the pad beside the door. Silently, it slid open and we stepped inside.

"Stay by the door," Brinley told Danec. "Count them all."

"Don't forget to count us," Slek said helpfully.

Danec gave him a funny look, but nodded.

A shout came from outside, followed by the sound of people eager to board.

"Five. Six."

While Danec counted, I moved further into the small vessel. Really just a shuttle, the pod consisted of a cockpit, storage bay and a section for seating. Off to one side was a small room full of bunks, perhaps enough for twenty to sleep. We'd have to sleep in shifts if we were here that long.

Brinley hurried into the cockpit.

Slek followed. "The pod should be ship shape, but just in case—"

I settled into a spot at the front, near the window and sat facing the door. On a small craft like this, we'd have little more than a first aid kit, but I would be ready if I was needed. Okay, *when* I was needed.

"One at a time," a voice roared from outside the door. "Ensign, how many passengers are in this pod?"

I squashed down in my seat and grimaced. With any luck, he would keep moving.

"Forty-six, sir," Danec replied.

"Three more over here. No, I said three. No more."

Three evacuees, two women and a man, hurried inside and took the last of the seats. When the door slid shut, I grimaced. It deepened when I saw Commander J'avet firmly on *this* side of the door, followed by Danec, who looked like he wished the floor would swallow him up.

"Fuck," I said under my breath.

The pod's engine started up. J'avet strode between the seats to the cockpit. He stopped when he reached me and scowled, but he marched inside.

The pod rose and glided toward the outer door. It slid first into a small section, where we stopped. A door slid closed behind us and the space doors opened.

"See, no being thrown out the airlock." Danec slipped into the seat beside me and put a hand on my knee.

"No, we're just flying out of it instead." I watched the side of the ship glide by before we moved out into space.

"The IF will send help." Danec sounded so sure.

"And if they don't?" I asked. I hadn't planned to die on a pod, out in space, with Commander J'avet present.

Danec shook his head. "Then we'll find a moon and wait."

"Oh good." That didn't sound much better.

"At least we both made it." Did he move his hand further up my thigh on purpose?

"Yes, thank goodness for that," I agreed.

Infinity grew smaller in the window. Once in a while, another pod would shoot out, or what looked like debris would float past.

I put my hand over Danec's and we sat there like that for a while, in silence.

10

"Any idea what happened?" Slek flopped into a chair and propped his booted feet on the one in front of him. He spoke softly, so as to not wake the twenty or so sleeping passengers in the bunk room and the dozen who curled up on the floor.

J'avet rubbed his hands over his face and pinched the bridge of his nose. "Sensors suggest an explosion. Cause unknown."

"There's nothing in that part of the ship to cause something catastrophic." Slek frowned. "Just a few conduits, computer banks... They should have been isolated automatically as soon as something went wrong."

"Assuming it was accidental," J'avet said. He

lowered his hand and exhaled. "We won't know until IF can get out and tow her to port."

"The closest port is Dendra," Slek said. "But it will take weeks for IF to get around to sending anyone."

J'avet nodded, then scowled at me as if he'd just realised I was there.

I ignored the look and aimed a question at Slek. "Is there any chance it was sabotage?"

In the corner of my eye, J'avet twitched.

"What?" he snapped.

Slek's brow furrowed deeper in confusion. "What do you mean?"

I tried not to wilt under the scrutiny of them and Danec, who sat beside me still, his hands on his lap.

I told them about my encounter with Jones in the corridor and his claim to have needed to check his watch. It had seemed halfway plausible then. Now it sounded ludicrous.

If J'avet's face wasn't already red, I think he would have turned maroon. His eyes flashed, literally. I swear I saw sparks of electricity erupt in his irises.

"You were aware of a potentially dangerous dissenter on board and you said nothing?" he growled.

Part of me wanted to shrink back from his anger,

but I didn't. Fuck him, I wasn't going to let him think I was weak.

I lifted my chin. "If I told security every time someone was angry at someone else for no apparent reason, I would waste a lot of their time."

J'avet's eyes narrowed. "Not everyone, just the ones who plan to destroy a ship and everyone on it."

I clenched my jaw. "I'm not telepathic," I said coolly. "Besides, Jones wouldn't be the first human who thought we should take better care of Earth and stand on our own two feet."

J'avet poked a thick finger in my direction. "And that's why Earth isn't ready to join the IF."

I wanted to swat his finger away. "That's not up to you."

"No. If it was, you'd be out, and all spacefaring craft ordered to stay away."

Slek looked as if he wanted to say something, but he closed his mouth. I guess he figured I could stick up for myself. He didn't seem to find J'avet intimidating in the least.

"You sound just like Jones," I told J'avet curtly. "Closed minded, just because people are different."

He spluttered for a moment before his expression turned cold. "I have no issue with people being different. I take exception to those who harbour resentment because other worlds are far more advanced."

"I wouldn't say far more," Slek said. Apparently he couldn't keep silent anymore.

J'avet glanced at him, then back at me. "If the IF finds an explosive device planted on *Infinity*, in the area of communications and navigation, with any trace of your friend on it, I will consider you complicit in the destruction of the ship."

Before I could do more than gape, he rose and stalked away, as far as he could go in such a small space.

"He's not my friend," I said to J'avet's back.

"Asshole-dickhead-prick," Danec whispered.

I held back a snort. The situation was bad enough without J'avet knowing we were laughing at him.

"Yeah," I muttered, then cursed softly to myself. "Is that even possible?"

"Finding you complicit?" Slek asked. He lowered his feet and leaned over to put a hand on my knee. "We'll be sure it doesn't happen."

"Yes, we will." Danec shifted closer and put an arm around my shoulders.

With both men so close, I was both confused and hot at the same time. Danec wanted to be friends, Slek wanted to take it slowly, and we were on a pod full of people. That didn't stop my mind from going into overdrive, fuelled by heated, pounding blood.

I swallowed and forced a half smile. "Thanks, guys. I suppose I should have said something, but Jones just seemed angry, not destructive. He wanted to go to Agus to make Earth a better place. Or so he said." Maybe I was so naive, I bought every word. I didn't want to think the worst of people. Well, most people.

I glanced toward J'avet, who now stood in the cockpit, speaking to Brinley in a low voice. I heard the name 'Jones' mentioned and Brinley nodded. No doubt J'avet put the word out to find the man. That was fair enough. With any luck, they would find him and he'd tell them I had nothing to do with what happened. Then J'avet could apologise—

Okay, I'm not that naive.

"We should try to get some rest," I said.

"Right. That reminds me." Slek pulled a screwdriver out of his pocket, rose, and crouched beside me. He undid the screws which held the row of seats in place and pushed it back as quietly as he could.

"If we're going to be here a while, we might as well get comfortable." He put the screwdriver away while Danec pulled out three spare pillows from the bunk room.

He tossed them into the empty space, then blushed. "Ummm."

"I'll sleep in the middle," I said, lying down.

Eyes wide, Danec lay down on one side, while Slek lay on the other. I faced Danec, who blushed even harder, before he placed a hand lightly on one of mine.

I gave him a soft smile, which he returned and made my heart flip.

Slek placed a hand on my hip, which made the *rest* of me flip.

"Good night," Danec whispered. His eyes flicked down to my lips. If I didn't know he wanted to be friends, I would think he wanted to kiss me. Instead, he swallowed hard and closed his eyes.

"Night," I said. Why was I so disappointed that he didn't kiss me? I was okay with being friends, wasn't I? Plus Slek's hand had moved to my ass. He cupped a cheek and gave it a squeeze.

Oh my goodness.

I closed my eyes and tried to sleep, while wishing Slek would move his hand down between my legs.

I fell asleep and dreamed of Slek, Danec, and J'avet, their hands all over me, mouths licking and sucking—

"Attention everyone."

I woke with a jolt. The pod's lights were on, suggesting it was morning, at least by someone's calculations. Considering the timing, I would guess J'avet's. Damn, dream him had been about to slide into—

"Pilot Brinley has informed me we don't have enough fuel to reach Denara." J'avet spoke from the front of the ship.

The evacuees let out a collective groan.

J'avet scowled at me as though the whole thing was my fault.

I hadn't even groaned. Except in my dream. I groaned a lot there. And moaned. Oh crap, had I moaned in my sleep? I glanced at Danec and Slek. They were sitting up, intent on what J'avet was saying.

I rubbed my eyes and tried to wake up more. I finally registered what J'avet said.

"We'll have to put down on Calig," J'avet said. "As most of you will know—" Again he glared at me, "Calig is unpopulated. The atmosphere is conducive to life, but resources are minimal. We will have to ration our food until the IF can reach us."

Danec raised a shaking hand. "Sir, will all the pods land there?"

J'avet nodded. "Each pod was allocated the same

amount of fuel. We will all make our way there and wait." He nodded and went to sit beside Brinley, who looked exhausted. He said something about taking a break and she nodded.

She rose and came to flop down beside Danec.

"I'm sorry, I tried to be sparing, but the pod really wasn't designed for so many people, so far from a port."

"We'll be sure to evacuate somewhere more convenient next time." Slek grinned.

Brinley snorted and lay down on his abandoned pillow. "Do that," she said with a smile. "The pod is on autopilot. I should sleep for a few hours. We won't reach Calig until tomorrow morning."

"Just enough time for J'avet to decide I should take a spacewalk," I said, with a frustrated sigh. "I wish I knew why he hates me so much."

"Because you're adorable and have people who care about you?" Slek suggested. He leaned down to give me a lingering kiss on my mouth.

"Right," Danec agreed. "He's just a grumble pants."

Slek and Brinley laughed and I made a face, but managed to smile at Slek.

"Thank you for thinking I'm adorable," I told him.

"I think you are t-t-too," Danec stammered. "Adorable, I mean, not a-a grumble pants."

"I can be both," I admitted. "I'm only human."

"Hey." Slek caught my chin with his finger and lifted it so I looked him in the eyes. "There's no such thing as 'just a human.' Humans are amazing."

"Even if a human might have been responsible for this?" I asked.

When Brinley gave me a questioning look, I told her about Jones.

"Oh," she said slowly. "He's odd and angry, but to do something like this? It seems extreme."

"Yes, well, tell J'avet that." I jerked an elbow in his direction. "After you sleep," I added, when she looked like she might get up and tell him off right now.

"If he wants me to fly this pod, then he better be nice," she declared.

"Are you planning to stop?" Slek asked, his expression somewhere between teasing and genuine curiosity.

Brinley barked a throaty laugh. "Of course not. I want to get us off this pod safely as much as everyone else." She sighed loudly. "Still, I wish we could make it further. Calig is off any shipping routes. Uninhabited, deserted."

"It sounds like paradise," I said. "Jones will love it." Assuming he made it off *Infinity* alive.

"There's no internet," Brinley groaned.

"What?" I feigned outrage. "No cat videos?"

"Not one," she agreed. "No online shopping either. Or chatting to friends. No social media."

"This is sounding better and better," I said. "But we won't be there for long."

"Right," Slek agreed. "The IF will have a ship on the way there already. They might even arrive before we do."

"That's right," Danec agreed. "Just in time for a hot shower and warm food."

Brinley groaned. "I hadn't even thought about showers."

"I guess you never camped as a kid?" I asked.

"Hell no." She grimaced, her tongue stuck out between her teeth. "I'm a city girl through and through."

"You're in for a treat then," I said, "if IF doesn't arrive first."

"Oh, you've camped?" Slek asked.

"No," I replied, "but how bad can it be?"

The side of Brinley's mouth drew back. "Let's hope the IF is there, waiting."

I agreed, but silently I was worried. What if they found Jones, but he claimed I was his accomplice? Nothing anyone said to J'avet would change his mind about me, I was sure of that.

He'd send me straight back to Earth and that would be that.

It might come to that, but I would fight before it did. For some reason I couldn't explain, some tiny part of the back of my mind wanted to change his mind about me. The fact he hated me hurt, although it shouldn't. No part of me should care what an asshole thinks, especially with Danec and Slek on either side of me.

Who needs you, J'avet? I thought.

Want, well, that was another thing.

11

We passed through the atmosphere of Calig without more than a bump. Still, a few gasped and exhaled loudly. Most aboard were awake now, huddled in groups with blankets around them, or nibbling on the dry ration bars and instant noodles which were all the pod was stocked with. Thankfully the pod was also stocked with enough clothes that no one was naked. Some still wore their pyjamas, but didn't seem too worried. At least they were alive.

"I'm looking for a place to land," Brinley said over her shoulder. "Everyone strap in."

She looked worried about something, but I couldn't ask right now, especially with J'avet sitting in the copilot's seat beside her.

Instead, I sat in what was my usual spot now,

between Danec and Slek. Slek had screwed the seats back in and checked on the rest of them, and the strapping. If we crashed, no one would get thrown through a window. Small mercy considering we'd probably die anyway. Of course, I had every faith in Brinley that wouldn't happen.

"Are you all right?" Slek ran a thumb over the back of my hand.

"I'm fine," I said. "We're about to land on a strange, alien world. What could go wrong?"

We hadn't seen any sign of the IF. If J'avet had received word from them, he wasn't sharing that information, at least not with me. I certainly didn't see a big ship in orbit, nor were we heading for a safe little ole pod bay. Nope, we were heading for a world that looked to have less water than Earth, approximately eighty percent if I guessed right, green continents, and huge frozen poles.

"From what I've read, Calig is like Earth was before industrialisation," Danec said.

I was coming to realise that. "Why hasn't it been colonised?"

"Few natural metals," Danec replied. "And it's out of the way from everywhere."

"Right. If you tell me there are dragons on this planet…"

He gave me a funny look. "Dragons?"

I shook my head. "It doesn't matter." Old sci-fi books from Earth's archives were a hobby of mine, but one they apparently didn't share. I would have to work on that.

One hand in Slek's, the other in Danec's, I watched out the window as the ground got closer and closer. Patches of green became trees, bushes and wide expanses of grassland. It was to the last that we headed.

"That's strange." Slek's forehead all but touched the window.

"What is?" I leaned over until my chest was pressed against his bicep.

"There should be other pods out there," he said.

I blinked. He was right. Pods had left *Infinity* after us, but we hadn't been the first off.

"They must be on some other part of the planet," I said.

"I suppose so." But he didn't look convinced.

I peered into the cockpit, but saw nothing but the back of Brinley and J'avet's heads.

"If they got eaten by dragons or space spores, I'm out of here," I muttered. Who knew where I would go, because I didn't have a clue.

"It'll be okay," Danec said. "The pod is equipped with laser rifles and I know how to use one."

He puffed out his chest until Slek said, "You point and shoot. Nothing to it."

"You have to...to aim as well," Danec said, obviously rattled.

"I'm sure it's not that simple," I said, addressing them both. Danec was trying hard and Slek didn't need to make him feel bad about it. We were all on edge, but we didn't need to take it out on each other.

Slek shrugged. "I guess, but if you really want a challenge, try a sonic bow."

"I w-won second place with a sonic bow when I was six," Danec said softly.

Slek looked impressed. "We should hunt some Parvoran boar some time. Good eating, but a bitch to shoot."

"That would be great," Danec said. "I've always wanted to try hunting those, but a permit is so hard to get."

"I have one. I use it when—"

I sighed to myself. We were about to land on a mysterious planet and they were talking about hunting pigs?

"Can I come?" I asked. If you can't beat 'em, join 'em.

"Absolutely. Wait until you see the sunset over—"

Something thudded against the side of the pod, hard enough to throw it sideways a kilometre or two.

"Hang on!" Brinley shouted.

The pod banked hard to the right and I was thrown against Danec. At least this time I wasn't thrown far. The harness held me for the most part.

Out the window I caught sight of a deluge of hail. No, not hail; rocks.

My heart stopped. Not rocks. Pieces of ship. My stomach twisted.

"The other pods," I said, my voice choked.

"There's too much debris for that." Slek's face was so pale he was almost lavender. "That looks like a whole ship."

"And the first of the pods," Danec said softly. "If they docked already."

"Oh no," I whispered. Tears sprang to my eyes. The IF must have been waiting and the first few pods had reached the ship. And then—

"What could have done this?" My eyes widened. And could it happen to us?

J'avet turned in his seat and looked in my direction. "Your friend Jones is on a pod behind us. Whatever did that—"

"Isn't him," I finished. "Then what?"

J'avet shook his head and turned back. That was probably the closest to an apology I would get from him. That didn't much matter now.

"I'm taking us in to land," Brinley said loudly.

"Everyone get ready for landing," J'avet said.

The pod banked the other way and headed for an expanse of grass. Chunks of debris rained around us, but only small pieces hit the pod.

When we landed, we did it in a skid. We slid across the ground for a hundred metres or more, then came to a stop just short of slamming into a trunk.

"Everyone out and make for the trees," J'avet ordered. He had already undone his harness and now threw himself at the door controller. It slid open silently and he stood to one side and waved everyone out ahead of him.

Someone took my hand, I couldn't even register who, and we ran.

The world around me became a blur of green until we reached a section of forest that was deep enough, the canopy thick enough, that we came to a stop.

"Trees aren't going to be much protection against space junk." Slek peered upward.

A crash sounded through the trees, followed by a rumble, then an explosion large enough to make the ground tremble under my feet.

"Neither was the pod," a Freytaurian woman remarked.

I grimaced in agreement. Had debris done that, or whoever had destroyed the IF ship? I shook my head and gulped. "We should find a bush to hide under."

"Or a cave," Danec said. "I've read about those."

"Yeah." I ducked down and peered through the trees. "Do you think Brinley—"

"She's fine," Slek said. "I saw her get off the pod. She won't be far behind us." I wish he looked as sure as he sounded.

"We should wait," I said. The forest had fallen into near silence, apart from the occasional shout, or thud. A tree a few metres away exploded into splinters when something hit it, but I couldn't see a cause, apart from more debris.

"We should find a cave," Slek said.

"Well fuck," I replied, "I forgot my map." I was also trembling so hard my hair bounced around my head.

Danec crouched beside me and wound his arms around me. "It's okay," he said softly. "I won't let any harm come to you."

"Who's going to protect you?" I asked with a sniff.

"You will," he said firmly. "And Slek. We'll look after each other."

Slek gave him an 'I can take care of myself, thanks dude,' look, but said nothing.

"We shouldn't stay here," Danec said. "Just in case."

I didn't ask 'just in case what?' Truthfully, I didn't want to think too hard about it. Not now.

"We should find some of the others," Slek said. "Commander J'avet, even."

"What about Commander J'avet?"

I never expected to be happy to see him, but when he stepped around a trunk and stopped a few metres away, Brinley beside him, I wanted to hug them both.

Instead, I rose and hugged her.

"Uh, we're craving leadership, sir," Slek said with both respect and irony.

"I'm certain you are." J'avet looked me up and down and, for the first time, I didn't see loathing in his expression. I saw no kindness either, but indifference was better than hate, at least in these circumstances.

"Or a map," I said.

J'avet rolled his eyes at me and I thought he

might snap. He spoke coolly instead. "This is an uninhabited planet, Nurse Wright."

"Edie," I said. "And uninhabited doesn't necessarily mean uncharted." I glanced at Brinley for support and she nodded.

"There might be maps, but unless we can access communication from a remaining pod—"

She didn't need to finish the sentence, we all knew what she was going to say. We might be alone here.

"We'll gather everyone and stay together," J'avet said. He pressed his watch and sent the location to each evacuee. If we couldn't communicate with the rest of the universe, at least we could communicate with each other. Until our watches died. Each only held enough power for a month, two at the most, before they needed to be recharged.

J'avet leaned against a tree, arms crossed over his burly chest. This was the first time I got a good, long look at him. His jaw was wide and stern. The fur on his face was so fine it could easily be mistaken for skin. His lips were thin but his mouth wide. His brow was heavy right now, in an impatient frown.

"Why would someone attack the IF?" I asked before I had any idea I was about to speak.

His frown deepened. "Apart from your friend, I

can only guess." He pushed himself off the trunk. "Not everyone is in favour of the IF. There are those without and within who would end the alliance altogether."

"Apart from humans?" I asked.

He stiffened. "There are others, yes." He turned away then and I knew that was all I was going to get out of him, for now.

Brinley was busy tapping away at her watch. She looked up and said, "I'm trying to warn the other pods. Two more landed about thirty kilometres east. They saw nothing but the tail end of the debris."

J'avet turned back. "It's possible whatever attacked the ship thought all the pods were aboard."

"Or they couldn't wait," Slek said.

"Or the pods weren't a target at all," I said. "Just an unlucky coincidence."

"Yes, that could be it." Danec seemed as eager to cling to a shred of hope as I was. "Just in the wrong place at the wrong time."

"Nevertheless, we'll be careful," J'avet said. "As soon as everyone is here, we'll go."

"Go where?" I asked.

"East," he replied simply.

Thirty kilometres through an alien forest, to meet up with the other shuttles, with who knows who or what possibly after us. Nothing could possibly go wrong, right?

I stepped closer to Danec and Slek moved to my other side, next to Brinley. In silence, we followed J'avet deeper into the trees.

1 2

WE SKIRTED the edge of the forest, alert for hazards amongst the trees and in the sky. Once in a while, in the corner of my eye, I saw movement. When I looked straight on, it was gone. Or maybe I imagined it.

"There's no such thing as invisibility cloaking devices, are there?" I asked Brinley.

She shook her head. "Not that I know of."

"Me either," Slek said. He seemed weary, his eyelids heavy. His head injury must be wearing on him more than I had suspected. He could use a doctor to assess him, or better yet, an infirmary.

"Are you all right?" I put a hand on his bicep as we walked. The muscles under my hand screamed 'invincible alien badass.' The lines on his face suggested mortal still recovering from an injury which might have killed him had he been far from medical help.

He covered my hand with his large one. "I'm okay. I could use a big chunk of Parvoran boar steak right about now."

J'avet glanced back over his shoulder at him. "Don't start thinking about food. We have a long way to go."

"Can't a pod come and get us?" asked an evacuee who walked behind us. He was tall and lean, with the yellow skin of a Centauri. He had given his name as Humar, but he seemed anything but funny.

"Not without drawing attention to whatever destroyed the ship and other pods," J'avet snapped.

"That could get us all killed," Slek said.

"So will starving to death," Humar said. "Are you sure we're going the right way?"

"Absolutely certain," Brinley said. "It's not that far. We've covered four kilometres already."

Humar groaned. "Only four?"

"You could always sit here and wait until someone comes for you," I snapped. "None of us are having fun here."

Danec murmured his agreement.

Humar grumbled something but fell silent.

I breathed out through pursed lips. "We could probably do with a break. Just five minutes. It's been traumatic for everyone."

I thought J'avet would refuse, but he stopped for a moment, then nodded. "Five minutes. Under the trees. Keep your eyes open."

"For what, sir?" Danec asked.

"Anything," J'avet replied smoothly. While most of us sat under the shelter of some tall trees, whose lowest branches were too high to reach, J'avet leaned against a trunk.

"Does he ever rest?" I whispered to Danec. I hadn't seen J'avet sleep on the pod either. An exhausted leader wasn't a good thing.

"I think he lay down for a little while," Danec whispered back. "On the pod, as we were going to sleep."

"Maybe he's an android." Slek grinned. "I bet he's the kind programmed to do any function required of him."

"Any?" I blushed.

Slek chuckled.

"He seems humanoid enough to me," Brinley mused. "Some people don't need much sleep."

"Others do." I nodded to where Humar lay beside a bush, eyes closed, breathing softly.

"Centaurians sleep more than they're awake," Slek said.

"That is incorrect," Humar said, without opening his eyes. "I am merely tired from a long shift and sudden evacuation."

"Right," Slek drawled.

"That's enough rest," J'avet said suddenly.

It was only four and a half minutes, but I didn't bother to say so. I pushed myself to my feet. A blur of movement caught my eye. This time I managed to focus for a second or two before it disappeared behind a tree.

"Please tell me someone else saw that." I pointed.

"I did," Danec said. "It looked like a sphere of..." He shook his head.

"Of stone," I said. "Black stone."

"Stone doesn't fly," Slek said. "It was probably some kind of metal."

"Oh good," I said sarcastically. "Are you sure this planet is uninhabited, because things like that don't just float around by themselves."

"No, they don't," J'avet said, his voice tight. "Do you think it saw us?"

I frowned in thought. "It did seem as though it stopped to check us out."

"We should hurry." J'avet gave the order to resume walking, but faster now.

"Do you think that's what happened to the ship?" I asked, my voice low so only Danec could hear.

"It's possible," he replied, "but whatever that was, it didn't seem aggressive. It looked like it was scared of us, or something."

"I am pretty scary," I agreed. I gave him a cheeky smile.

He smiled back, but his eyes were laced with worry. "If that was a scout of some kind…"

"Then they've been watching us for hours," I finished for him. "That's the first time I got a good look, but I'm sure I've seen something floating around before now. I wasn't sure if I imagined it, or maybe it was a bird or a bat, or…" Some other alien species I was unfamiliar with.

"Me too," Brinley said. "Whatever they are, they're trying to avoid being seen."

"Until now," I said.

"Or you seeing it was a coincidence," she said.

"I suppose it could be," I conceded. I had the niggling feeling it wasn't.

"Maybe we shouldn't be going this way," I said loud enough for J'avet to hear.

He stopped and turned around, his customary

scowl in place. "What do you suggest?" he asked in a tone which clearly indicated he didn't much want to hear it.

I chewed my lip. "I don't know. Deeper into the forest?"

He sighed. "Unless that's a couple of bags of rations under your shirt?" He looked about ready to grab one of my breasts and find out.

I crossed an arm over them. "I have half a ration bar in my pocket."

"Then we continue this way, but stay alert," he said curtly. "Although, some of us could stand to miss a meal or two." He gave me a pointed look, then turned and stalked away.

My jaw dropped, and I know my face turned bright red.

"Why you fucking—" I started forward, but Danec and Slek each grabbed one of my arms and held me back.

"Don't, Edie, it's not worth it," Slek said.

"Yeah," Danec agreed. "You'll be in trouble when we get off this planet."

"If we do." I strained against them for a moment, then sagged. "You're right. he's not worth it." Asshole-dickehead-prick didn't cut it. He was a stone cold bully. I would be happy when I never had to see him again.

"We should keep going," I said.

The guys hesitated for a moment, then let go of my arms.

"It's not okay." I stomped in J'avet's boot tracks, which gave me some satisfaction, small and petty though it was.

"No, it's not," Brinley agreed. "You could always file a complaint later."

"With who?" I spread my hands. "Management is a bit scarce out here."

She giggled and almost forced a smile out of me. Almost.

"He has a commanding officer out there some-where," she replied.

"General Taffin," Danec said. "She's the only human of that rank in the IF."

"Let me guess, he resents her?" I asked bitterly.

"I-I don't know," Danec admitted. His eyes widened. "Sh-she's pretty intimidating."

"Men and their fucking egos," I muttered. I didn't care what his reasoning was. His bruised ego was his problem, not mine.

"You know what," I declared, my voice a bit louder. "I'm not sharing any of my half-a-ration bar with him."

"Good for you," Slek said. His voice sounded strange enough for me to glance at him. He looked back, a deep frown on his handsome face.

"What is it?" I asked.

"I think we're being followed," he said softly.

"There are other evacuees—" Danec started.

"No," Slek said abruptly. "Something else. Something… I don't know."

"Evil?" I suggested.

He glanced at me and a small smile flashed across his face. "Hopefully not. Excuse me." He trotted forward to J'avet, but his movement seemed forced, tired. "I think we're being hunted," he said, loud enough to be overheard.

J'avet scowled and gave a curt nod in response. "Ensign Danec, Engineer Slek, you and Ensign Humar make your way parallel to our position. Try to get around whatever is behind us."

"And then what?" I demanded.

J'avet ignored me. "Assess the threat and report back," he said to Danec.

"Yes, sir." Danec's eyes were wide and full of regret as he glanced at me, then hurried away to the north.

Slek grimaced, but followed, a surly Humar on their tail.

"Continue on," J'avet ordered, without so much as a glance at the rest of us.

I gave Brinley a worried look. We linked arms and stepped as quickly as we could behind the commander. I hated the idea of being anywhere near him, but if something came at us, maybe I could duck fast enough that it would eat him first. That thought felt so good, I found myself smiling.

"Having fun?" Brinley asked, clearly not sure if she should tease or be concerned.

"No." I shook my head. My mouth moved, but I couldn't explain without J'avet hearing and getting pissed off even more. "It doesn't matter."

"If you say so," she replied.

"Quiet," J'avet snapped. "Unless you want what's tracking us to find us."

Us? No. Him? Right now, I wouldn't mind if it bit off his head and licked his bones clean.

I fell silent anyway.

If I hadn't, I might have missed the crack of a twig behind us.

I tapped J'avet on the shoulder to tell him and had the petty satisfaction of seeing him jump.

He glared at me, but I jerked a thumb behind me.

He peered toward the trees and squinted, then waved us toward a clump of bushes. "Get down," he hissed. He all but shoved us over and pushed himself down so close to me his arm was pressed against mine. I wanted to jerk away, but I stayed perfectly still, frozen except the pounding of my heart.

Another crack sounded, closer this time. Whatever it was, they were trying to be careful, trying not to to make a sound. If it wasn't for the dry twigs, I wouldn't have known anything was there at all.

I swallowed hard to push down rising panic and ducked down further.

Leaves in front of us rustled. At first I thought it might be the wind. The second time, I knew there was something there.

Beside me, Brinley trembled, and knew I did the same. Did J'avet tremble too, or did I imagine that?

The leaves rustled again, closer still and a voice swore.

"Slek?" I started to stand, but J'avet pulled me down so hard I landed on my ass. I exhaled out my nose at the pain and glared at him.

He mouthed, "Do you want to get us killed?"

I glared, but shook my head. Of course I didn't, but I could have sworn…

"Where did they go?"

That was definitely Danec's voice, whispering loudly.

J'avet blew out a breath and rose. "We're over here," he said, his voice only slightly louder than Danec's.

"Oh." Slek stepped into view now and rubbed his forehead. "There was nothing there. No sign of anything either."

"You must have been hearing things," J'avet said accusingly.

"I guess so." Slek looked around carefully. "I could have sworn..."

"You were mistaken. We've wasted enough time on this. We'll walk for two more hours, then find a place to make camp."

I shivered at the idea of spending a night here, but the look on Slek's face made my blood run cold. He frowned at the trees back the way we'd come and shook his head, obviously not convinced we weren't still being hunted.

13

THE SUNSET WAS STUNNING, but night fell rapidly. Without flashing computers or corridor lights, the darkness was unsettling.

"There's no way I'm going to imagine a monster creeping up on us," I said sarcastically.

"The moon should rise soon, according to Brinley," Danec said. "Oh. Do you see that?"

I jumped. "Where?" I glanced around and listened, but heard no enormous footsteps, no ominous sound of a giant alien slug sliding toward us, no buzz of people-eating bees. What? I've seen a lot of science fiction movies, okay?

"Over there." If he pointed, I couldn't see it. I could barely make him out as it was.

"Please say it's an underground bunker full of

cheese," I pleaded. I ate a bite of my ration bar, but it wasn't close to enough. "Above ground would be good, too."

"Um, no, I don't think so. Look over there, on the lake."

Before dark, we had stumbled across the small body of water, nestled half in and half out of the trees. When I say stumbled, I mean one of our party had stepped out of a clump of bushes, right onto the bank. Only the quick-thinking companion who grabbed her arm kept her from falling in.

J'avet crouched beside the water and tested it with his watch before he declared it safe to drink. He wasn't the first to try it, but neither was I. That dubious honour went to Danec, who J'avet waved forward as he stepped aside.

I might have told him to fuck off, but Danec knelt, drank, and lived to tell about it.

I squinted at the water. "The plants floating on the surface are phosphorescent." In daylight, they looked like some kind of waterlily. In the gloom, they glowed a soft green. "It's so pretty."

The slowly rising moon cast a silvery glow, which illuminated his face. He looked right at me. "Beautiful," he said softly. Surely he was only talking about the plants.

In spite of myself, my mouth went dry and I had to swallow. "Should we go and take a closer look?"

"Hmmm? Uh, yes." I couldn't see him blush, but for some reason I was sure he was. "I'd like that."

I followed him around the edge, keeping a safe distance from the water, and watching for fallen logs and mutant slugs.

I stepped around a patch of grass and slid on muddy ground. I windmilled my arms, but Danec grabbed my hand before I fell and kept me upright.

"Thank you." My heart pounded so hard it left me breathless.

"You're welcome." His voice was rough. He didn't let my hand go again. Instead, we walked like that, close together and hand in hand, to the other side of the lake.

Here, the leaves glowed brighter, but still soft on the eyes. In the centre of each plant, the lilies glowed as well, each a different shade of pink, purples, blue, and yellow. Even white here and there.

The glow increased as the flowers, closed at first, gradually opened their petals out to embrace the night air and the ever brightening moon.

"Oh my goodness." I inhaled the scent of the blooms which grew stronger the wider they spread their petals. The smell was warm and heady, intoxicating. "We should go for a swim."

I took half a step before Danec pulled me back to him.

I didn't realise he was going to kiss me until his mouth was on mine. His lips were soft, but hungry, as though he wanted to devour me in one mouthful. His tongue went searching and I opened my mouth to him. He licked my lips and his tongue felt rough, unlike any other I had tasted. No, not rough, textured.

In the next moment, it was gone and him with it. He stepped away and rubbed a hand over his face.

"I'm sorry. I'm s-so-sorry," he stammered. "I shouldn't have done that. I-I—"

I closed the gap between us and put a hand on his muscular forearm. He felt like rock under my fingers.

"It's all right," I said. "I liked it." I more than liked it; I wanted more. What I couldn't understand was what he wanted. He had my head spinning this way and that and I didn't want to do that anymore. Whatever he had to say, I needed to know.

"Are you sorry because you just want to be friends?" My tone was more blunt than I intended, but the words were out there. Regardless of the outcome, I had made the first step.

He gazed toward the lake. "No," he said finally. "It's because I thought you wanted that. I mean, you called me friend. I'm all right with that, I just…"

"I only called you that because that's what I thought you wanted," I said. Right now, my body throbbed like crazy and my mind buzzed. Was he saying he also wanted more?

"From the first moment I saw you, I hungered for you," he said, his voice low and rough. "I was prepared to respect whatever you wished, even if it was friendship, just so I could be near you. Every time you let me hold your hand, I was happy just to do that. That sounds so pathetic." He exhaled loudly

"No," I told him, "that sounds sweet. You've helped me get through the last day or two. Hell, only a few minutes ago, you stopped me from falling into the water." I didn't want to think of the glare I would get from J'avet if I returned to camp, my clothes soaking wet.

"I would do anything for you." He took my hand again and drew me to his hard, warm body.

"You were even the first to drink the water," I pointed out.

His body shook with laughter. "Even that. If I

died, well..." He paused and inhaled through his nose in a way that suggested he was about to broach a difficult topic. "Slek—"

Ah. That certainly was difficult. "I like him too," I admitted, even as I pressed my head against Danec's chest. "I know that's not—"

Normal?

Sane?

Sensible?

"Ideal."

"It's a-all right," Danec said. "I'll be here when you figure out what, or who, you need. As long as it takes. But I hope you choose me." His arms closed around me and squeezed, gentle but firm.

"I make no guarantees." The scent of him was more heady than the flowers. I leaned back and looked up at him.

His blue face was a riot of different shades in the light from the flowers. Slowly, he lowered his mouth to mine and kissed me gently. This was nothing like the first kiss, but the fire it sent through me was hotter than ever. I wanted to throw him down into the darkness, tear off his clothes, and feel him sink deep into me.

We broke apart and I nestled my face into his chest again.

"I feel safe with you," I said. More than physically safe. He was sweet and kind and I knew if he broke my heart, it wouldn't be intentional. He probably didn't have a mean bone in his body.

Unlike— No, I wouldn't think about J'avet just now. He didn't deserve to spend a moment inside my head. Not even a nano-moment. Was a nano-moment even a thing? Whatever, he could stay out.

"Good, I want you to feel safe. We'll get off this planet and make it to Agus, no matter what."

"And if we don't, we'll have to colonise and populate Calig," I said more lightly than I felt.

He chuckled. "Yes." A couple of heartbeats later, his body stiffened. "Edie, I don't think we're alone"

"There's about forty-eight other people beside the lake," I said.

"Not them," Danec said. "Behind you."

I turned slowly. There, in the bushes, were several sets of shining eyes. Every so often, they blinked both lower and upper lids at the same time.

"Hello?" I said tentatively. "We mean you no harm." With any luck, they meant us none too.

The response was a rustle of leaves and one individual rose. The multiple pack of abs and broad arms suggested he was male. His skin shone silver in the glow from the flowers, although interspersed with other other colours.

Another form rose beside him, this one with bare breasts and hair which fell past her waist.

"Harm," the woman said as if feeling out the word.

"No harm," I said quickly. "Peace. Um." I looked to Danec for help, but she seemed to understand.

"Peace," she echoed.

"So much for uninhabited," I muttered. To the pair I asked, "So you live here?"

"Here." It was the man who spoke this time, his voice a pleasant rumble.

"Yes, here, Calig." I pointed to the ground.

He cocked his head. Long silver hair fell to one side, almost as long as the woman's. He said a word I didn't understand.

"Dirt?" I guessed. "Uh, the ground is dirt," I agreed. "The whole planet is." I had no idea where to go from here, or if they understood a word I said.

"Iritauri," Danec said suddenly.

Both the man and woman's head jerked to look at him. The woman nodded excitedly and pointed toward herself. "Iritauri. Selvia." She pointed to the man, "Landu."

Danec pointed to himself, "Danec." Then to me, "Edie."

"Eeedee," the woman drew out my name and nodded.

I smiled, then out of the corner of my mouth, I asked, "Who are these people?"

"The Iritauri," he said. "Or Iri. They were a race of people who shared Freytauri."

Landu spat on the ground.

I wrinkled my nose. "Past tense?" I asked.

"They were persecuted. Many left. Those who didn't…" His voice was laced with regret for an event which had probably happened before he was born.

"And here they are," I finished. No wonder they hid from us. They probably thought we'd come to finish the job.

"I'm sorry your people were treated badly," I said. "Can they understand me?"

"Your watch should have a translator on it," Danec said. "Turn on Iritaurian and it'll do the rest."

I did as he said. "Testing." The word spoke the word again, but this time in a different language.

Landu chuckled and repeated the word.

My watch responded. "Testing."

This would be slow and clunky, but better than nothing.

"So, you live here, on this planet?" I asked again.

"Yes, yes." Salvia nodded. "We crashed here. Calig is home now. For three generations."

"Oh." I hoped we wouldn't be here for that long. "I suppose that means there's food around."

"Lots of vegetables and fish." Landu pointed toward the lake. "There's good eating when the moon flowers bloom."

That was good to know. Food was that close, we just had to catch it. Of course, my knowledge of how to do that was limited to not at all.

"Maybe we can trade," I suggested. "Food for… Well, we must have something you'd want."

Salvia gave a curt nod. "Trade."

"Great," Danec said. "Maybe you could teach us to fish in return for my watch?"

Before he could slip it off his wrist, Slek spoke loudly from a few metres away.

"Who are you speaking to?"

I put my hand up as a sign to wait, but Selvia and Landu, eyes wide, ducked back down and all of the eyes melted away.

"Oops, sorry," Slek said. "I didn't realise there was anyone here." He peered toward the bushes, but they fell still. The Iri were well and truly gone.

I sighed and told him about the encounter.

"Iritauri," he said in wonder. "I thought they were extinct. Bare breasts, did you say? That's a local clothing tradition I could get behind." He eyed me speculatively.

I rolled my eyes at him. "I would say you first, but you'd have your shirt off before I could blink."

"If you did it too, I would," he replied. "I thought you two had come over here to go skinny dipping." He didn't seem bothered that I might swim naked with another man.

"We came to see the flowers," Danec said. "Do you think we should follow them?"

I peered into the darkness. "I hate to say it, but I think we need to tell J'avet."

"After we skinny dip?" Slek asked.

"Instead of that," I said regretfully.

Slek and Danec both sighed. I did the same a moment later. Here I was, beside a stunning lake, on an alien world, with two guys hotter than the nearest sun, both of whom wanted to get naked with me, and I was going to report to the leader of our group instead.

I must be crazy, at least a bit. At this point, I might come if one of them looked at me the right way.

"Come on, we should get back," I said. "Before he

thinks we deserted and decides to have us all arrested." Good luck with that, since we had no security officers with us, but once we got off Calig, that would change. There was no point in giving him another excuse to be an asshole.

Slek slipped his hand into one of mine and Danec took the other. They shared a look, which seemed to be an understanding of some kind. They would respect me and my wishes until I decided between them.

If I did. That might be harder than getting off this planet. How could I possibly make a choice between two guys I was falling for?

14

J'AVET MASSAGED the bridge of his nose with his fingertips. "Tell me again what you saw? Iritauri?"

"If you've never heard of them—" Slek started.

J'avet glared at Slek past his hand. "I've heard of them," he snapped. "Their genocide is a source of shame for the people of Freytauri, and the IF itself. Had they intervened sooner..." He waved a hand. "And you claim they're alive and well and living on Calig?"

"We don't claim anything," I said coldly. "We saw them. Spoke to them. They're as real as you." But a lot more friendly.

"Near blooming moon flowers." His tone matched mine. "A known hallucinogen."

I wanted to slap the smug look off his face.

Instead, I shrugged. "We're just telling you what we saw. Believe it or don't believe it, that's up to you. Now, if you'll excuse me, it's late and I'm tired."

If I had a shred of sympathy for him, I might admit he looked tired too, but I didn't. I gave him a glare through narrowed eyes and stalked away to the tree where Brinley sat.

I threw myself to the ground. "He's such a moth-erfucking twatbag."

"I assume that's a bad thing?" Danec lowered himself down beside me.

I half snorted, half choked a laugh. "Yeah, it is."

"You'd let him near your mother?" Slek asked. Clearly he understood the irony in the comment, because he smiled and one eyebrow twitched upward.

"Over my dead body," I muttered. I lay down on my side and sighed. "We really should get some sleep."

Brinley nodded. "Yes, we should." She put her hand over a yawn.

The guys got comfortable on either side of me. Danec, who lay in front of me, gave me a smile before he closed his eyes.

Slek rested a hand on my hip.

I closed my own eyes and, for a long while, I stayed like that, but my mind spun faster than light.

What if J'avet was right, and we had imagined the Iri? It wasn't the first time I've pictured muscular, alien men. I might be horny enough to imagine bare breasted alien women too, although my taste didn't usually run that way.

I shifted my hip to get more comfortable.

"Are you all right?" Slek said right beside my ear.

I rolled over to face him. "I can't sleep," I whispered. The only sounds around us were Danec snoring softly and Brinley murmuring what sounded like coordinates in her sleep.

"Need some help?" Slek's hand slid down my hip, to my thigh.

I bit back a moan. After a moment, I bent my knee to let him slip his hand between my legs.

He moved, slow and feather-light, to brush against the front of my pants. He rubbed again, firmer this time, and tickled my neck with his tongue. Like Danec's, it was textured, enough to drive me wild.

His teeth grazed my skin, up to my chin before he claimed my mouth with his. His lips fastened on my lower lip. He sucked it gently, then gripped the skin between his teeth and bit down lightly.

He pulled away long enough to whisper, "I could eat you up." With one hand, he undid the front of my pants and pushed his fingers inside. He was a tight fit, but he found the front of my panties and rubbed with a firm, confident touch.

In a heartbeat, I was wet as hell and rocking against his fingers. I had to press my lips together to keep from screaming, or begging him for more. We lay on the edge of the group of evacuees, but still so many slept close by.

With his other hand, Slek pushed up the front of my shirt, just to the bottom of my bra. He reached in and cupped a breast. My nipple hardened against his palm.

I wanted more. So much more.

He tugged the side of my panties aside and slid the tip of his finger against my folds.

I quivered.

He pulled his hand out of my pants and wiggled them down my hips, just enough so they were out of the way. He left my panties, except to again pull one side out of the way. He grazed the whole of his hand over my clit, from the tips of his fingers to the heel.

I let out a tiny whimper.

He pressed one finger gently inside me. At the

same time, he peeled back my bra cup and massaged my nipple with his thumb and forefinger.

My breath was coming in tiny pants now. For a guy from another planet, he knew his way around a human woman's body. I knew the physiology of many different species had similarities, but sexual pleasure wasn't something they taught in nursing school.

He slid another finger inside and another, until I felt almost full. The heel of his hand rubbed my clit while his fingers massaged my insides.

I bucked against him, faster and faster.

He leaned over to slide the tip of his tongue over my nipple. His tongue split in two and each side went over and around my sensitive peak. Double the fun.

Just that small touch drove me close to the edge.

He caught my nipple in his lips and suckled for a moment before biting down gently.

I quivered and whimpered again.

"Slek," I whispered.

"Mmm?" he said while his teeth grazed across my breast, nibbling here and there. He bit hard enough to leave a mark and I had to bite back a scream of pleasure.

MAGGIE ALABASTER

"You like that." He moved to another place and bit again.

"Please—" I didn't know what I was asking for, until he exposed my other breast and nibbled on it too. "Yes."

The next time he bit me, I came, hard and fast against his hand. "Yes... Slek..."

I rocked, eyes squeezed shut until he milked every bit of orgasm out of me. Only when I was finally still and panting, did he still his hand and raise his mouth from my breasts.

"There. That might help you sleep." He worked my bra cups back into place and tugged my shirt down. He drew his hand out of me last, brought his fingers to his nose and sniffed.

"I didn't know human women were so scented." He stuck his fingers into his mouth and sucked. "And delicious," he said around them.

My hand hovered near his groin. "Do you—"

He pulled his fingers from his mouth and shook his head. "I'll keep. We agreed not to rush."

"Okay." I pulled my pants back up and did them up. "Thank you." I was slightly disappointed. I had seen his cock and looked forward to playing with it. On the other hand, exhaustion started to seep into my body, down into my bones.

Anticipation never killed anyone, right?

He hooked an arm around me and drew me closer, him the big spoon, me the smaller one.

I wiggled against him for a moment, then nestled down, safe and warm in his strong arms.

"Do you believe we saw them?" I asked sleepily.

"Do you?" he asked. He sounded equally weary.

I thought for a moment. "Yes, I'm certain we did. If I was going to hallucinate, I would see a big pile of chocolate. Or pizza, wine, and a movie."

Slek chuckled. "Hunger will do that."

"Yes, it will," I sighed. I looked forward to a good meal after this. At least we had plenty of water from the lake to sustain us tonight and tomorrow morning.

"If you had imagined it, you wouldn't have seen the same thing," Slek pointed out.

I stiffened for a moment before I forced myself to relax again. "You're right, we wouldn't." Part of me wanted to march up to J'avet and tell him that, but the other ninety-nine percent of me was perfectly comfortable here. Besides, picking a fight now wouldn't achieve anything.

I squeezed my eyes tight and let my mind wander. The lake, the flowers, Danec's kiss, the Iri... It was all real, I was certain of it. That led me to wonder what it was about the Iri that the Freytauri felt the need to eradicate them. Race? Language? Disputes over land?

I was about to ask Slek when he started to snore loudly. I moved my ear further away from his mouth and exhaled through my nose. My last thought before I slipped off to sleep was that I must be the last person awake in camp.

I wasn't the first to awaken when dawn broke over this part of Calig. That honour went to Humar, who woke the rest of us with his shout.

"We're surrounded!"

15

"I *TOLD* him the Iri were real," I muttered. I sat up, pulled my hairband from my wrist and tugged my curls into a hasty ponytail.

"We believed you," Brinley assured me.

I flashed her a quick smile and got to my feet.

Humar's declaration about being surrounded was a slight exaggeration, but there were quite a few Iri standing around our camp. Each was armed with a long, slender bow. None were nocked, but the Iri all had a quiver of arrows on their backs. I would bet J'avet's pension they could have them ready to shoot in a heartbeat or less.

"We want to speak to your leader." Selvia's words came through my watch, translated for those close enough to hear.

Those who couldn't, muttered amongst themselves. "What did they say?"

"I don't know, I think we might be breakfast."

"Shit."

I rolled my eyes and stepped forward.

"Hi, Selvia, it's me, Edie." My watch spat my words out in Iritauri.

She turned toward me with a proud tilt of her head. "You are the leader?"

"No, I am." J'avet stepped forward. Judging by the way his watch translated his words too, he cottoned on quickly.

I had to give him some credit for that.

"What do you want?" he asked warily.

"We want to trade," Selvia replied.

I took my eyes off her long enough to look around at the rest of the Iri. A few metres from Selvia stood Landu. He gave me a nod, then went back to scanning the encampment, his whole body tensed, ready.

Right. Just because Danec and I were harmless didn't mean the rest of the evacuees were.

"We don't have much," J'avet said. "We had to evacuate our ship. Our escape pod was destroyed."

Selvia tilted her head at him. "My symbiont says you have access to resources not of this world."

Symbiont?

J'avet's brow jerked upward.

I glanced back toward Slek and Danec. Neither looked surprised in the least. Was this the reason their people hunted the Iri? What form did this symbiont take?

J'avet's reply tugged my mind back to the moment.

"We have access," he said carefully, "but only when we can reach the other pods, safely."

Selvia nodded. "We will be your escort and guides. We brought food." She half turned and waved toward the trees. From between the trunks came a handful of men and women. Each carried a basket. Every one was laden with loaves of bread and fruit.

My eyes widened and my stomach rumbled so loudly I was sure J'avet would hear.

"That's very good of you," he said, his tone still wary.

I could almost see him thinking, wondering what they really wanted. I wondered the same thing, but maybe they were just being nice. Surely that was possible? If not, then what did they want in the way of off-world resources? It may be nothing more than wine or chocolate. Truthfully, it wasn't really my problem. The IF would deal with them and give them whatever they needed once we were safe. And we got to eat. That sounded like a win-win to me.

"Help them distribute the food." J'avet waved at Danec and Humar. Danec nodded, but Humar looked horrified at the idea of going anywhere near them. Hunger, or the need to follow orders, won in the end, and he took a basket of rolls and took them around the evacuees.

I grabbed one, still wonderfully warm and soft, and bit into it. While I chewed, I caught J'avet watching me. Then everyone else. I deliberately swallowed and took another bite.

When I didn't die, the others started to eat.

If Selvia and the others noticed, I saw no sign, their expressions were closed doors. That in itself made me uneasy, but the bread was so tasty I put the reservations aside for now.

I finished my roll in about three seconds and grabbed a piece of fruit from the basket Danec had passed around, but which now sat at his feet. It looked like an apple, but with bright orange skin.

"Any idea what this is?" I asked.

Danec had one of his own on the palm of his hand and was examining it with careful curiosity. "I have no idea. It must be native to Calig."

Landu still stood back from us, but he had one of

the strange fruit as well. He bit into it and chewed happily.

"If it's safe for him," Danec said, "it should be safe for me." He bit into his and nodded his appreciation of the taste.

Before I tried mine, I asked, "What did they mean about the symbiont?"

Danec swallowed in a hurry and coughed a couple of times.

I patted him on the back and waited for him to regain his breath.

"Some of our people chose to accept a symbiont to be their host," he said finally. "Others of our people…"

"Didn't like the idea?" I finished for him. I wasn't sure I blamed them. I wouldn't want to be a host for, well, anything. "So there's a parasite of some kind living inside them?" I whispered.

"Something like that, yes," he agreed.

I eyed the closest Iri, a woman around my own age. Like the others, her breasts were bare, but her hair was shorter, the ends cut ragged. I suppose they didn't have access to a hairdresser down here. Maybe all they needed from the IF was a few good pairs of scissors. Somehow, I thought there might be a bit more to it than that.

I bit into the fruit. Juice flooded into my mouth like a bite of honey, but not as sweet. While I chewed, I watched the Iri woman for some sign, any sign, of a worm, or slug, or whatever might share her body. Nothing rippled under skin, or burst out to announce itself. She looked like an ordinary alien, with silvery skin.

"This fruit is good," I said. I ate it down to its core and tossed the remains in the direction of the trees. It wasn't chocolate, but I could happily live on that and bread for a few days.

"Yes," Danec looked like he might say something, but he just tossed his core in the same direction as mine and grabbed another.

"Are you all right?" I asked.

His eyes widened, but he looked toward the ground. "Um…"

"Okay." I crossed my arms over my chest. "Out with it."

"I…You and Slek—"

I grimaced. "You heard that?" When he nodded, I grimaced harder. "Sorry, I thought you were asleep."

"I was. And then I wasn't."

"We didn't mean to wake you." Especially like that. We should have crept off into the bushes or something.

"You didn't," he said quickly. "It's okay, it's not about that." He blinked slowly. "Did you choose him?"

My breath came out in a rush. "No," I said quickly. "I would have told you if I had." I understood where he was coming from though. If I'd woken to find him with his hands down the pants of another woman, I'd assume he'd made up his mind too.

I licked my lips. "It's just... I needed... And wanted... I still want to see where we go." I put a hand on his arm. "I'll understand if you don't feel the same way. If you want to find someone else."

"I don't want anyone else," he said in a hoarse whisper. I had noticed he'd hardly glanced at the Iri's bare breasts, at which some of the evacuees hadn't stopped staring.

"If I have to share you with him, I'll do it. But—"

"But what?" I asked.

"If you choose him, please tell me. And if you need... Want... I'm here too. I might not be as experienced as Slek," he blushed, "but I can learn."

My heart melted a little more. I grabbed his hand and pulled him in to kiss his cheek. At the last moment, he turned his face and my lips grazed lightly over his.

"If J'avet sees—" I started.

"If he doesn't like it, I'll quit," Danec growled. "You're more important to me than the GASP."

Now I blushed. "Don't throw your career away because of me," I told him. "What would you do anyway?"

He shrugged. "I could work cataloguing the IF database of books. Don't worry about me, I'll work out something."

"In the meantime, we should hand out more fruit." I leaned to pick up the basket and we walked around the group of evacuees until it was empty. Once or twice I caught J'avet watching me, but I pretended not to notice. We'd be off this planet and away from him soon enough.

I hoped.

"All right," J'avet called out suddenly. "Finish stuffing your faces and prepare to make your way out of camp in an orderly fashion. Follow the Iritauri leader." He said the words like they left a bitter taste in his mouth. Was he still angry with me because he'd said we hadn't seen the Iri, only to be proven very wrong? If so, then he would have to get over himself, whether he liked it or not.

16

"I DON'T THINK we're going the right way," Brinley whispered.

We'd been walking for two hours now, but I began to wonder the same thing.

"It's east-ish," I said, unconvinced.

"It's north-east," Danec said. He walked beside me. The worry on his face was a look I hadn't seen on him before.

I wanted to ask where we might end up if we kept going, but any reply would only be a guess.

"Should we speak to J'avet, or ask the Iri?" Brinley asked. Her expression matched Danec's.

I chewed my lip. I wasn't going to speak to J'avet if I didn't have to.

"I'll ask Landu," I said finally. "He seems nice enough."

"I'll come with you," Slek said. "I haven't spoken to an Iri up close."

I hesitated, then nodded. "All right, come on then."

He grabbed my hand and we hurried to catch up with the silver skinned alien.

"Landu," I greeted when we were close enough. I smiled and looked as friendly as I could, which didn't look suspicious *at all*.

"Eeedee," Landu replied. He gave me a nod without slowing and shot Slek a speculative look.

Slek's grip on my hand tightened and he drew me closer.

I raised my eyebrows at him, but he was looking at Landu with undisguised wariness.

I cleared my throat. "Um, so. We thought we were going east. This is, um, not east."

Landu frowned until my watch translated. "Not east," he agreed.

"Why?" Slek asked. "We need to go to the pods."

"Selvia said we're going this way," Landu replied in a tone which suggested we shouldn't argue.

That might have worked on his people, but not on me.

I stopped and planted my fists on my hips. "Why? What is this way?"

Landu stopped too and cocked his head. "That is for Selvia to say."

"I'm asking you," I insisted.

He hesitated for a moment, his face expressionless. "Shardu is this way," he said and kept on walking.

"Wait." I grunted in exasperation and dragged Slek along to catch up. "What the hell is Shardu?"

"Shardu," Landu said, "is where we live."

"But we need to go to the pods," Slek said. "You're supposed to take us that way." He looked like he might be tempted to punch Landu in the face if we didn't get some straight answers soon.

"I have no more answers," Landu said simply. "We will be in Shardu soon."

"Then will we get answers?" I asked.

"If Selvia wishes to give them," Landu agreed.

Slek swore under his breath. "Not good enough," he snapped.

"I can do no more," Landu replied indifferently. "Selvia will say no more until we arrive in Shardu."

Now I swore, because asking her was exactly what I was planning to do next.

"And what if we don't want to go to your city, or

whatever it is?" Slek asked. "We might just continue east by ourselves."

Without a word, Landu put a hand on his bow.

"Or we could just go with you to Shardu," I said quickly.

Landu lowered his hand and nodded.

"So much for friendly," I muttered. "Beware of aliens bearing gifts." We should have known them giving us food was a part of some kind of plan. Okay, I think we did know, but we were too hungry to care at the time. I could blame J'avet for letting us fall into this trap, but then I'd have to think about the asshole. My day had already taken a turn for the worst without that.

"I won't let any harm come to you," Slek promised. "If they so much as touch a hair on your head, I'll—" His face turned dark purple and eyes flashed with anger.

"You won't do anything which might get you killed," I said firmly. "We've come this far, we can deal with this."

He looked like he might argue, but he nodded and the anger faded from his features. "You're right. Danec and I and the other Freytauri will need to be especially careful. The need for vengeance can last for generations."

I hadn't thought of that. Now I did, the fruit soured in my stomach. "I hope that's not what this is about."

"If it is, we'll handle it. Just make sure you and the others get off safely."

"I always like to be safe when I get off," I assured him.

He chuckled. "Good girl. Me too." He sighed. "I hope I don't regret not asking you to suck my cock last night."

"Priorities," I teased.

He grinned. "What can I say? I've waited a long time to feel your mouth on me."

"We only met a couple of weeks ago," I pointed out.

"Did we?" he asked. "I feel as though I've known you all my life." He slung an arm over my shoulder, and didn't remove it until Brinley and Danec caught up.

We told them what Landu said, and they both frowned.

"So we're prisoners?" Brinley asked.

"In a manner of speaking, yes," I said. "They're outnumbered, but we're unarmed. So far they don't seem to want to do anything to us." If they wanted us dead, we'd be dead. "If we just go along with what they say, we might be okay."

We might also be lunch, but I didn't think that was the case. I personally didn't think I would be that tasty, but that was a matter of opinion, I suppose.

I glanced around at the weary faces around me, some looking concerned, others oblivious. Past the closest handful, I caught the look on J'avet's face. His mouth was a tight line, eyes narrowed and snapping with their usual bad temper. There was something more though. He understood the situation. If I didn't know better, I would think he had always been aware of it. I suppose he had; he was an asshole, not an idiot.

That idea made me angry. He knew, but he'd let us all walk into this anyway?

I huffed a breath through my nose. Not two minutes earlier, I pointed out we weren't armed. He'd had no choice. That realisation did nothing to make me feel better.

I shivered.

Danec put an arm around me. "It'll be all right. I won't let them do anything to you."

I gave him a watery smile for making the same promise Slek had.

"Thank you. I'll make sure nothing bad happens to you too," I told him. "Or Slek, or Brinley."

She gave no sign that she was bothered by me getting the attention of two guys. In fact, she seemed happy for me. Once in a while, I caught her smiling when one of the guys held my hand, or said something sweet. A lot of girls would get jealous, even bitchy, but not her. That made me like her all the more.

Brinley grinned. "Yeah, take care of the one who can fly us off this rock."

"You're not the only pilot," Slek said, speaking as though he was teasing a younger sister.

"Just the best," she said tartly. She even stuck out her tongue at him.

He stuck out his in return.

I stared in fascination as he spilt the tip of his tongue in two, until it looked like a fork. Both sides curled upward, so he looked like he was sticking up two fingers at her.

I laughed.

He grinned, then rejoined the sides of his tongue together before drawing it back into his mouth.

"Do you think we should be more mature?" Danec suggested.

"*Pfft*, maturity is overrated," Slek said. "So I've heard anyway."

"Who do you know who is mature?" Brinley asked. "Apart from Danec. And maybe J'avet."

Slek rubbed his chin. "No one I can think of," he admitted.

"Exactly," Brinley said.

"Shhh," Danec said suddenly.

"What—" I stopped to listen.

"There's nothing—" Slek started.

"Yes there is," I said quickly. In the distance, engines thrummed. They rapidly grew closer.

"Friend or foe?" Brinley wondered out loud.

I shook my head. I didn't know. At least until a pod appeared over the trees, followed by another. And another.

They passed overhead and kept on in the direction we were going. My eyes followed them the entire way over and my heart followed them down to the ground.

"Keep walking," Selvia ordered. Her expression offered nothing, no hint of her thoughts on seeing the pods.

For some reason, that gave me chills. I rubbed my hands up and down my arms and stomped on behind Landu. If my eyes could bore a hole in the back of his head, they would.

"Shardu," he said after about another twenty minutes of walking.

"I figured," I muttered. Shardu was a collection of buildings made from sheets of metal. Some bore signs of having been a ship of some kind. Others looked like flooring or walls. Several buildings had two stories and balconies made from catwalks.

"Reduce, reuse, recycle," I muttered. "Is that why you destroyed the IF ship?" I directed the question to Landu. "For housing parts?"

He half turned his head toward me. "We destroyed nothing."

"Right." Then why did I sense a 'yet' at the end of his sentence?

"This way." Selvia waved to the open field beside the town where the pods were neatly parked, side by side. Six of them. Their passengers stepped out into the sunshine, followed by several Iri armed with bows and even a knife here and there.

"This can't be good," Brinley said softly.

Silently, I agreed.

The passengers were directed to sit in a spot under the shade of a wide tree with white flowers dotted here and there. Under other circumstances I might have appreciated its beauty. Now though, I sat where I was told and searched the gathered crowd.

There. Scared and angry, but alive, Jones sat near the edge of the group, apart by choice or because no one would sit closer, I don't know.

"What do you want with us?" a Garvian woman called out. Her tentacles dropped with obvious exhaustion.

Selvia ignored her and spoke in low tones to two or three other Iri. They nodded and bustled off, presumably to do as she'd asked.

"Food will be provided," she said. "Do as you're told and no one will be harmed."

"Right," someone said, disbelievingly.

If Selvia heard, she ignored it. She nodded to another Iri and disappeared into one of the buildings.

I started to look for J'avet, but soon found him sitting directly behind me. I caught his eye and nodded toward Jones.

J'avet followed my gaze and nodded. "Your accomplice," he said, but sensed he didn't believe it anymore.

I snorted anyway. "Hardly. You can ask him yourself."

"I will," J'avet agreed. He glanced at the Iri closest to us, rose and kept low as he made his way over to Jones.

Acting on instinct, I followed. I didn't need to look over my shoulder to know Danec, Slek, or Brinley followed. Possibly all three.

"Jones." J'avet plopped down beside him. "Did you plant a bomb on *Infinity?*"

That was blunt.

Jones blinked, the confusion genuine. I didn't need to hear his answer to know he hadn't.

"Of course not," he hissed. He nodded toward me, cold fury on his face. "Did she tell you I did?"

"She suggested you were acting strangely in the part of the ship which later exploded," J'avet said.

Thanks for throwing me right under the shuttle. I glared at him, then at Jones.

"You were acting funny and you hate aliens," I pointed out.

"Not enough to potentially kill myself," Jones retorted. "And certainly not if I knew we'd end up here." He shot daggers at the Iri with his eyes. his mouth was set in a line so tight his lips turned white. "What do they want with us anyway?"

"Hostages," Danec said. He had followed and now

sat on the other side of me. Slek and Brinley were on the other side of him.

"Obviously," Jones snapped. "But why?"

"I think we're about to find out." J'avet nodded toward the closest building.

"Shit."

1 7

My curse was followed by the sound of dozens of nocked bows, all pointed toward the gathered evacuees.

The Iri moved amongst us, directing some toward the building Selvia had gone into, and others to the one beside it. Still others were pointed toward a third building.

Selvia herself reappeared in front of us, a long, slender tube held in one hand.

I was no expert, but I knew a weapon when I saw one.

"Laser hand cannon," Slek muttered. "An oldie but a baddie."

That didn't sound good.

"You are their leader," she said to J'avet.

He nodded and rode steadily to his feet. "I am."

"You, a pilot and these Freytaurians," she shot Danec and Slek a disgusted look, like they smelled of something nasty, "will come with me."

Before I could twitch, much less argue, she waved her cannon at me and Jones. "These two as well," she stated.

Jones shot to his feet. "I'm not going anywhere with you."

Calm to the point of coldness, Selvia raised her cannon toward him. A beam of orange light shot out the end. It struck him in the chest, then enveloped him entirely. He threw his head back to scream, but then disappeared as if he'd never existed.

My breath caught in my throat. I'd seen people die before, but never like that, with no warning at all.

"Shit," I whispered.

"Now you understand," Selvia said. "Obey and no one else will be harmed."

A thousand questions tumbled around in my head, but for once I kept my mouth shut. Selvia's demonstration was more than enough to convince me to contain my patience.

J'avet looked furious, but when Selvia gestured us

toward the closest pod, he nodded for us to walk that way too.

As if I had planned to do otherwise.

"If you have further thoughts of escape," Selvia said, "we have other weapons, all trained on the others in your landing party. Their continued existence depends on all of you."

I thought that might be the point in separating us all. Divided, it would be harder to rise up against them.

"I'm not sure there's enough fuel to get far," Brinley said as we stepped into the pod.

"My people have worked to drain the others. The combined fuel is on board."

"Oh." Brinley nodded. "That would work."

I wouldn't even pretend to be surprised they knew how. The Iri were clearly more advanced than they let on. The bare chests must be a life choice, not a lack of resources. Good for them, I suppose.

Selvia nodded. "Fly us up into orbit."

"There's the small matter of someone up there taking aim at ships above this planet," J'avet pointed out.

"They are of no concern," Selvia replied.

I frowned at her and caught Danec and Slek with identical looks of disbelief on their faces.

"We'll be concerned when they shoot at us," Slek muttered.

Selvia waved us toward the seats and sat behind us.

"Does anyone else think this is a bad idea?" I whispered.

"I have a bad feeling about it," Slek agreed.

A dozen Iri stepped onto the pod, along with Humar, an Agusian woman, and four more Frey-taurians.

The doors slid shut behind us and Brinley turned on the ship's engines.

"They sound healthy enough," Slek said after a moment. "I saw no sign of damage to the exterior."

"That's good to know," I said.

Danec was quiet, his skin pale.

I took his hand. "Are you all right?" I asked.

"I'm sorry," he whispered. "I should have done some-something."

"You would be dead too if you tried," I reminded him. "At least this way we have a chance." How, I didn't know, but we'd come up with something.

The pod jolted and rose off the ground. Out the window I watched the last of the refugees ushered inside the buildings. Some stopped to stare, but were soon hurried on. Was Kalvix amongst them? I hadn't seen her, but I had been busy with Jones. I hope she was all right. I hated to think the doctor had died on *Infinity*, or one of the pods.

"Uh, Iritauri leader," Brinley said awkwardly. "There's a ship in orbit. I'm pretty sure they've seen us. They aren't IF."

Selvia nodded and rose. She pointed her cannon at Slek and Danec.

"You two, into the cockpit," she ordered.

I opened my mouth to argue, but when she aimed her cannon at me, I shut it so hard my teeth clicked. I raised my hands and slumped in my seat.

"Contact them," Selvia said. She gestured for Slek to sit beside Brinley and Danec stood beside him, in front of Selvia.

"Tell them we're a Freytauri pod," she ordered. "Liberated from the IF."

Slek gave her a funny look, but cleared his throat and did as she asked.

The closer we got to orbit, the bigger the ship became.

"IF design," J'avet muttered. "But an older one."

"Older as in supposed to be scrap, but currently flown by pirates?" I asked.

He glanced toward me as though he'd forgotten I

was there. "Pirates, or those who don't believe in IF ideals," he said.

"Like Jones?"

J'avet looked grim. "Far worse, if I'm guessing correctly."

I thought quickly. Why would Selvia want the ship to think we were Freytauri and not IF? Unless...

"Rogue Freytaurians?" I guessed. "Ones who want to finish off the genocide, but the IF won't let them?"

"Possibly." His eyes unfocused and he thought aloud. "Their plan may have been to slow us down, to keep us busy fixing *Infinity* so they might get it done before we reached orbit. *Infinity* was evacuated more quickly than they anticipated."

"Is it possible they tried to sabotage the engines first?" I asked. Maybe Slek was pushed after all. "If that's the case, then..." The blood drained from my face.

"There's a Freytaurian or two willing to kill us to finish their job, and they may be on this pod." J'avet looked toward the cockpit.

"It's neither of them," I said firmly.

He looked like he might say something more, but the communicator in the cockpit crackled.

I leaned forward to hear the rogue's response.

"Nice work," I couldn't see them, but their accents sounded like Danec and Slek. "Can you prove it?"

"We're both Freytaurian, aren't we?" Slek spread his arms. I was sure he was grinning, but could only see his back.

"Who else would be bold enough to steal a pod right from under IF noses? As a bonus, we have hostages. More on the planet and a colony of Iritaurians, ripe for the slaughter."

Did he have to sound so convincing?

Apparently J'avet thought so too, because he gave me a sidelong glance.

I didn't want to draw Selvia's attention, so I refrained from giving him a one finger salute.

The comms went silent for a moment.

My heart stopped. I was sure the ship had cut contact and was about to open fire. We would be the proverbial sitting ducks.

This was the moment my father would say to kiss my ass goodbye, but I wasn't ready to do that yet.

My hand in my lap, I pressed a couple of buttons on my watch.

I looked up to see J'avet's eyes on me. He nodded, then turned back to the cockpit.

The comms crackled. "You're cleared for

boarding in pod bay three. We'll send a contingent to meet you."

In other words, 'come on board, but we don't trust you as far as we can spit you, yet.' Fine, whatever got us on board. Once there, I'd figure out a way to prevent us from getting killed.

"Thank you." Slek cut the comms.

"Back to your seats," Selvia ordered. "Don't get too comfortable, You'll be needed soon enough."

Visibly troubled, both guys rose and flopped back into place next to me.

"Out of the frying pan, into the fire," I said.

"I wish we *had* hallucinated them," Danec said. "Or better yet, run."

"We might have, if we'd been believed," I said to the back of J'avet's head.

He turned and scowled at me. "Save your 'I told you so' for when we get out of this."

"I prefer to say it now," I said easily. "We might not live long enough for me to do it later."

He rolled his eyes and turned away.

"Fine. If we live through this, you can tell me why you hate me so much."

The ship loomed closer in the windows, especially the gaping hole in the side that must be the pod bay door. It sat open like a giant maw, ready to eat us whole and crunch our bones.

With that cheery thought in my head, I gripped Danec's hand and braced myself.

The pod slipped neatly through the door and into a long, well lit tunnel that led deeper into the ship.

The space door closed behind us and I immediately felt a bit heavier. Presumably the ship's gravitation was heavier than the pod's. I felt stuck down to the floor.

Danec grunted and shifted uncomfortably. Evidently he felt it too.

I looked past him to Slek, who seemed uneasy for different reasons. My tongue darted over my lips. "Those things you said—"

He set his mouth in a line. "I didn't like it any more than you did. I'll say whatever I have to to keep us alive."

"I know," I said quickly. "But you knew what they wanted to hear. You don't seem too surprised to find Freytaurians out here who—"

He cut me off. "I'm not. They usually stay away from IF space, but I knew they existed."

Danec looked at him in surprise. "I had no idea."

Slek smirked. "No offence, but you're barely off your mother's tit. Figuratively speaking. If you were any more innocent, you'd still be back in school, playing mathematics games on your tablet."

"I'm not that innocent," Danec muttered angrily.

"We shouldn't fight with each other," I snapped. "Slek, what are these Freytaurians capable of?"

"Besides running around the galaxy, destroying IF ships, and hunting Iri to kill? Just about anything, I'd say."

"They wouldn't hesitate to kill you," Selvia said. She'd walked back and forth through the seats and evidently heard at least the last bit of our conversation. "They would likely have their pleasure with you first." She cast an eye around the pod. "Anyone who isn't a Freytaurian. Perhaps even those who are, but who disagree with their ideals."

My stomach turned at the idea of any of us being violated like that. Even J'avet.

"I will die before I let him touch me," Humar declared loudly.

Selvia turned a cold smile on him. "You may get that chance."

She would kill as easily as any Frey-T rogue.

The pod bumped to a stop beside another couple, both a lot older and more battered this one. The rogues would probably welcome it with open arms, if not its passengers.

"We're here." Brinley sounded relieved, but anxious. If all Selvia needed was a pilot, she may have no further need for my friend.

Selvia nodded and waved for Brinley to step out of the cockpit.

"Close the door," she ordered, waving her cannon at Brinley.

Brinley nodded and hurried to comply.

"You two, to the pod's door." Selvia gestured to Danec and Slek. "You as well," she said to the other Freytaurians. Everyone else, in front of me."

I hated the idea of turning my back on her, but I complied.

Brinley, her pretty face creased in the kind of frown my mother would have told me off for, stood beside me. She grabbed my hand and moved in close.

"It'll be all right," I said softly. "We'll get through this."

"I know," she replied. She didn't seem convinced.

I gave her a small smile as the pod door opened.

Six, maybe eight Freytaurians, skin ranging from pale blue to deepest purple, stood with weapons raised at us. Every one, man and woman, wore clothes that had seen better decades, with patches here and there to cover the multitude of holes.

They certainly looked like a bunch of pirates. Hungry ones, from the way they eyed us all.

A cold shudder passed through me. For the first time, I really wasn't sure we'd survive this.

"Step down slowly," one ordered. Evidently he didn't notice Selvia until she stepped off the pod last. When he did, his eyes widened and he raised his blaster.

Before he could fire, Selvia pulled a tube out of her pocket and tossed it onto the floor. When it hit, the tube shattered. Hundreds of tiny, glittering particles were dashed across the floor.

"Oh, shit," Slek muttered.

18

"WHAT THE—"

The particles drew together like a swarm of bees. Then, as though on some unseen signal, rose like a wave toward the rogues.

One aimed their blaster and fired. The shot hit the centre of the wave and made a hole, but it closed over again a moment later.

"Nanobots," Danec said.

His word took a moment to sink in.

Nanobots.

The symbionts.

The Iri didn't have slugs or bugs inside them, they had nanobots.

The wave lurched toward the Freytauri, who

hurried back, blasters still aimed, although they must know the futility of them now.

The tail end of the swarm broke off when the swarm stretched too far. The new pack headed in the other direction, toward Danec and Slek.

"No!" I cried out.

Someone grabbed my arm and tugged me back toward the pod. In the back of my mind, I registered J'avet.

"We can't leave them behind!"

The swarm caught up with a rogue who almost slipped in his haste. They crawled up his body like ants on a honey pot, until they reached his face. His eyes went wide. They slid into his ears and up his nose. His whole body stiffened. His arms flew out to either side and his back arched. The striking shade of blue faded out of his face and became a softly mottled silver.

He relaxed.

He smiled. His blaster dropped from his fingers.

My blood went cold. "Danec! Slek!"

J'avet pulled me hard and Brinley was right behind him. Selvia stood aside now, the other Iri arrayed behind her. Her expression was one of triumph. Her smile grew when the swarm engulfed another man.

I caught sight of Humar. He backed away from the swarm. His face was a mask of terror. He all but shoved a fellow evacuee in front of the swarm in his haste to reach the pod.

The evacuee, a Freytaurian woman named Kaeran, almost fell into the swarm from the force of his shove.

Danec reached for her, but missed her hand by a hair.

She staggered and kept her feet, but disappeared from view behind the silvery mass. She squeaked out a choked scream, then fell silent like the others.

A section of the swarm broke off and headed toward Humar. Just when I thought it would engulf him too, it split in two and went around him and hovered in the air before it headed right for Slek.

"It just wants Freytaurians," J'avet guessed. "Everyone, back in the pod! Ensign, Engineer—" He broke off as another evacuee was swallowed up.

"No!" Selvia growled. She aimed her cannon at Danec. "All Freytaurians will accept a symbiont."

"Personally, I'd rather die," Slek remarked.

She swung the cannon toward him. "You will be a host."

I held my breath. What I was about to do, could have me full of symbiont, or dead, or—

Without stopping to think for a moment longer, I broke away from J'avet and threw myself at Selvia. With her attention on Slek, she didn't see me coming. I barrelled into her hard enough to knock her back a few steps.

I grabbed for the hand cannon and tried to pull it from her.

Of course, someone full of nanobots and used to manual labour was a lot stronger than me, but it gave Brinley time to act. While Selvia and I wrestled, the small pilot darted past Slek and Danec and scooped up the rogue's dropped blaster. With no hesitation, she turned and aimed at Selvia.

The shot hit her full in the arm, a fingertip away from my hand. The force sheared through her wrist, severing her hand.

The smell of burnt flesh in my nostrils made me gag.

While Selvia stared in horror at her stump, I dove for the cannon and grabbed it before the other Iri could blink.

I waved it at them. "Move away from the pod. Everyone, get inside." I had an idle thought and aimed the cannon at the nanobots who were closing in on Danec.

"No," Selvia groaned.

That was all I needed to hear. I fired the cannon toward them. The blast cut a swathe through them.

For a moment they paused and I started to think they were out of commission. Slowly, gradually, they moved toward each other, closing the gap and re-forming. Their numbers were fewer, but I suspected just as dangerous.

The cannon on them and the Iri, I hurried toward the pod, waving everyone inside with my spare hand.

I fired another shot at the swarm which made a last lunge at Slek before the door closed behind us. A second before it did, I caught sight of the rogues. They were all Iritauri now. The smiles on their faces chilled my bones. They and the swarm turned and headed deeper into the ship.

"We need to get out of here," I said.

Brinley gave a sharp nod and hurried into the cockpit.

"A weapon doesn't make you the leader," J'avet said, but his tone wasn't as cold as it had been.

"Are you sure?" I asked, but I let my hand drop and the cannon with it. To aim it at anyone, even as a joke, wasn't funny.

"Certain." He took the cannon from my hand and patted my shoulder. Without another word, he retreated to the cockpit and left me to tremble before Slek and Danec gathered me in their arms and led me to a seat.

"I don't know if I should be happy to see you, or angry you didn't tell me anything about nanobots," I growled, but I was glad to be alive.

"I wasn't certain," Danec said. "The history books were never precise."

"No one has used nano technology for a long time," Slek added. "It was banned over fifty years ago."

"I wonder why," I said sarcastically. "I suppose that's the reason your people tried to kill the Iri. It wasn't because of the people, but because of the nanobots."

"I assume so, yes," Danec agreed. He cupped my cheek and leaned in to kiss my mouth lightly. "That was the bravest thing I've ever seen."

"Yes, you saved my ass," Slek agreed.

"I acted without thinking," I admitted. "I couldn't let her kill you, or let you be assimilated."

"Either way," Slek looked sly, "I owe you a lifetime of orgasms."

I laughed softly. "Totally worth it then."

"Strap in!" Brinley shouted.

The pod lifted off, turned in a slow circle and headed back the way we'd come.

We moved slowly, or at least it felt like it. We approached the first set of doors and stopped. A lifetime passed, but it wasn't even a minute before the door slid open.

"It's there to keep pods out, not in," Slek said.

"Oh." I still watched the door carefully until it was fully open, then left out a soft breath when it closed behind us. "One to go."

I didn't know if it was the ship or us which shook for a moment.

"Slek?" I asked slowly.

"Yes, Edie?" He quirked an eyebrow at me.

"Do ships of this age have a self-destruct?"

"Ummm. Yes. Yes they do."

"Shit."

The pod shook again, but this time I was sure it was only us.

"I, once again, have a bad feeling about this," I said.

"Me too," Danec agreed.

We approached the space doors and stopped. Like the last time, they took their time in opening. The longer it took, the more convinced I was we'd have an army of newly minted Iri chasing us.

"Danec, are the Iri dead?" I asked.

"No, they're under the control of the nanobots. From what I've read, they can still think for themselves, they just can't go against the nanotbot's programming."

"I see," I said. "I would hate to be at the start of the zombie apocalypse."

Slek gave me a funny look, but Danec smiled briefly. Apparently I needed to educate Slek on movies from Earth.

The space doors finally slid open on the beautiful expanse of space and the glittering stars.

The relief was short lived.

Between us and the glittering stars, something else glittered. It trickled down the side of the window, then moved to the edge as though seeking a way in.

"We have company," I said loudly. I shoved Danec and Slek toward the middle of the pod and faced the window. "I guess they won't suffocate in space?"

"No," Slek replied. "But we will need to get them off somehow."

"An interstellar car wash isn't a thing, I suppose?" I asked.

"No," Danec replied. "And we can't fly too close to the sun and burn them off. And we can't—"

Together we said, "Throw them out the airlock."

I would have laughed. Maybe later I will. Not now.

"What kills them?" I asked.

"Time," Slek replied slowly. "They'll power down if they don't find a host."

"How long?" Danec asked.

"Uhhh. About three weeks," Slek said regretfully.

"We don't have three weeks." J'avet had stepped out of the cockpit to listen. "We have maybe five days of oxygen. No more."

"I said *about* three," Slek muttered, "It could be less."

"Less than five days?" I asked.

"No," he admitted.

"Unless you have a solution..." J'avet stared him down.

Slek frowned. "The cannon Selvia had might do it."

"It's in *here*," I said. "The nanobots are out *there*."

Slek rubbed the side of his nose. "Unless we can rig that up to the forward array and..." He wandered off toward the cockpit, talking under his breath about numbers and technical specifications.

"In the meantime, stay away from—" J'avet's eyes

widened at what he saw in the opposite window, behind my shoulder.

I turned and gaped.

The rogue's ship flashed with warning lights. I braced myself for the wake from the explosion if the Freytauri had engaged the self-destruct.

From one breath to the next, the lights turned off and the ship began to move away.

I creased my brow. "Either the Freytauri kept control, or—"

"Or the Iritauri are leaving orbit," J'avet finished.

Barely a minute later, another ship appeared in the window. This one was more distant, but coming fast. It was followed by another and another.

"It's about time," I muttered.

J'avet smirked.

"What?" I asked. "I sent the distress signal hours ago."

"They got here as soon as they could," he said.

Before I could respond, he turned away.

He was right, but the nanobots were quickly increasing in number. I didn't want to think about how. They didn't seem to feed on each other, and there was no material floating around, except the pod. They would either eat their way in, or they would eat the pod around us, until we were sucked out into the vacuum.

Maybe now I should kiss my ass goodbye. Instead, I moved to lace my arm around Danec's.

"It'll be all right," I said. I wasn't sure if I was trying to convince him or myself.

The pod shuddered as the nanobot swarm started to tap at the windows.

"Yes, it will," Danec said. He sounded as terrified as I felt.

The IF ships drew closer, but they seemed slow, too slow. The rogue ship increased speed.

"If we get out of this," I started.

"We will," Danec said. "We'll be fine. The IF is here. Slek is working. We'll be okay. We'll be okay."

The tapping became more insistent. I felt the overwhelming need to pee.

"We're going to die!" Humar shouted. His voice was raw with stone cold fear, the likes of which I had never heard before. It accurately summed up what I was feeling myself.

"We'll be fine," I snapped, in spite of myself. "Keep calm."

Tap.

Tap.

Tap

Crack.

Oh shit.

I squeezed my eyes shut and leaned into Danec. At least my life would end beside someone I cared about.

"When this is over, I want to watch movies and eat popcorn," Danec said.

"You like popcorn?" I asked.

"I've never had it, but I've heard about it," he admitted.

"Okay, we can make that happen," I said.

A moment later, the engine stopped dead and silence fell over the pod. Silence deeper than the universe itself.

Then the tapping increased and the window went black, covered entirely with tiny nanobots.

"Shit," I muttered.

19

THE LIGHTS in the pod went out. We were plunged into darkness.

I waited for my eyes to adjust, to find some hint of light to see by. They didn't. The darkness was absolute.

My heart raced. Panic rose inside me, along with a scream which threatened to tear from my throat.

Danec held me closer and whispered something.

I couldn't hear it over the pounding of blood in my ears and the ringing from the utter silence.

"What?" I asked.

"I said I like you," he repeated. "A lot."

"I like you too." Was now really the time for this? I supposed it was, we might never get another chance. "Very much."

Before he could respond, the lights came back on so bright I blinked hard and shook my head.

"There," Slek said. "I've rigged the cannon to..." He shook his head. "It doesn't matter. What does matter is that we have one chance at this. And..."

"And what?" J'avet asked, eyes narrowed at Slek.

"And it could backfire and blow us all up," Slek said lightly. "But if this doesn't work, we're probably screwed anyway, so I say we give it a shot."

"That's your professional opinion?" J'avet asked.

"Professional. Personal. Guy who doesn't want to end up infested with nanobots." Slek sounded indifferent, almost sarcastic, but fear flashed in his eyes.

"I say we do it," I said.

J'avet glanced back at me, quirked a brow, then nodded at Slek.

"Do it." To the rest of us, he said, "Sit down and strap in. This could get rough."

"It isn't already?" I asked under my breath.

Danec snorted his agreement, but strapped in beside me and draped an arm over my shoulder.

"In three," Slek said loudly.

Beside him, Brinley's face was pale with anxiety, but she looked hopeful. If anyone would understand what Slek had rigged up, she would. Her expression gave me hope too. Maybe we'd be okay.

"Two."

J'avet's eyes were on the window. The odd lights in his irises flashed briefly. Maybe he was part machine too, I mused, but I was almost certain he wasn't.

Humar squeaked with fear, but I had no sympathy for him. The nanobots wouldn't have touched him. He hadn't needed to push the Freytauri woman into their path. If he hadn't, she might be here with us.

I sighed softly. He wasn't to know, I suppose.

"One." Slek slammed the heel of his hand down onto a button.

The cannon, attached to a cable of some kind, lit up. Or at least, a series of buttons down the side did.

For several heartbeats, I was sure it was about to explode and kill us all.

Something outside the pod flashed and Slek let out a whoop of joy.

The flash was followed by another flash, further down the ship, then another. The swarm on the window thinned.

Thinned further.

With the fifth flash, the last of the nanobots fell away and floated off into space.

"If they don't bump into any ships, they'll deactivate and become harmless," Slek said.

With any luck, that would be exactly what happened.

"We've taken a lot of damage," Brinley said. "Those nanobots were hungry."

I shivered.

J'avet nodded and pressed a button in front of him. After a crackle, a face appeared on the comm screen.

"Commander J'avet, you're alive." Did the Centaurian woman on the comms from one of the IF ships sound disappointed or did I imagine that?

"So it would seem," he said dryly. "You need to go after the other ship before they get too far for interception."

An Agusian man looked over the woman's shoulder. He bore the same rank insignia as J'avet. His antennas twitched toward the screen. "Thanks for the tip, commander. We're already in pursuit."

As he said that, two of the IF ships broke away from the other, which remained on a course straight toward us.

"Did someone chew on the pod?" the commander asked.

"Yes, Zarex. I got hungry waiting for you," J'avet said sarcastically.

Zarex grinned. His eyes were warm with humour.

"You always were impatient," Zarex said.

"You were always late," J'avet retorted.

"Not this time," Zarex said. "We got here just in time to see you blow nanobots off your pod with an old-fashioned laser hand cannon. I didn't think those things existed anymore, after they were, you know, banned." Zarex cocked his head and looked slightly accusing.

"It wasn't ours," Slek said helpfully. "We were just using it to save our asses."

"I'll brief you when I'm on board." J'avet looked like a man who had used up his last fuck. I didn't blame him. I was running short on them myself.

"Copy that." Zarex moved out of view.

The Centauri woman nodded at the screen. "The pod bay is ready, Commander J'avet. Please proceed."

"I hope this old girl has enough left in her to make it that far," Brinley said. She leaned over to press a few buttons and we slipped through space, toward the welcome sight of the open space door.

A moment before we slid inside, I caught a

glimpse of an explosion in the distance. I couldn't be certain, but I assumed the IF ships had caught up to the rogues and blew them out of space. Freytauri or Iri, they were a threat to the IF either way, but the idea of all those deaths made me shudder.

I swallowed hard. "It looks like you get popcorn after all." I tried to speak lightly when all I wanted to do was drink a bottle of some kind of alcohol and eat a whole pizza while hiding in a blanket fort. I mean, we've all felt like that, right? I felt like that several times in the last twenty-four hours.

"I'm just happy we're safe," Danec replied.

I exhaled through my nose as the space doors closed behind us. "So am I," I said. "That's all that matters right now."

Slek stepped out of the cockpit and slipped into the seat beside me.

"If it wasn't for you, we'd be bare-chested and silver skinned by now," he said.

"If it wasn't for you, we'd be dead," Danec told him.

"That's true," Slek said, with no humility whatso-ever. "Just an old engineer's trick."

"Does that mean you're an old engineer?" I teased.

"Ouch," he laughed. "I'm just a boy. Not as young as Danec, of course."

Danec looked annoyed. "I'm not that young."

Slek leaned over to slap him on the shoulder. "No, I just hope you're old enough to deal with it when Edie chooses me."

"Who said I'm choosing you?" I asked.

Slek's confidence didn't slip an iota. "You will. Why wouldn't you, I'm adorable."

"Danec is pretty cute too," I said.

Danec looked embarrassed, but pleased. "You think I'm cute?" He shot Slek a triumphant look.

"You *are* cute," Slek said. "So are kittens. Edie needs a wildcat to keep up with her." He made a gesture with his hand, like a cat batting the air.

The pod slid through the second set of doors and landed in the pod bay with a bump which might have thrown me off my seat if not for the harness.

Slek grabbed the seat in front of him to stay in place.

"Sorry," Brinley called over her shoulder.

"At least we're alive," Slek said.

"Yes, everyone out," J'avet ordered. "The IF will want to look over the pod. Engineer, stay with the pod. They'll be sure to have questions."

Slek looked disappointed, but nodded. Before I could step toward the door, he grabbed me to his firm body and planted a searing kiss on my mouth.

His tongue split and one side slid over my lips, while the other slipped inside my mouth.

I melted a little before he pulled away.

"Just something to keep you warm for a while." He gave Danec a challenging glance which clearly said, 'game on' before he pushed me gently toward the door.

I stepped outside and gasped. The outside of the pod really did look like it had been chewed.

Chunks of metal were gouged here and there. In more than one place, it seemed so thin I don't know how it hadn't ruptured.

"I didn't realise how close we came," I said in a whisper.

"Too close," Danec agreed. His eyes were huge.

"Oh my goodness." Brinley stood beside us. Her face was pale with exhaustion and horror. "I'm not sure I want to fly a pod again." After a pause, she added, "At least not today."

I smiled softly and gave her a quick hug. "I'm glad you did fly us. You did an amazing job."

"Awww, thank you." She looked pleased. "I need to find where I can clock my hours. They all count toward my qualifications."

"Ah, the intrepid pod crew." A door at the end of the bay slid open and Commander Zarex stepped through, followed by a contingent of security and a couple of engineers.

Zarex's gaze scanned us all. I probably imagined his eyes lingered on me for a moment longer.

"J'avet, I'm sure this will be an interesting debriefing," Zarex said.

"I would imagine so," J'avet agreed. "We should start by sending pods to rescue the other refugees from Calig." His voice lowered and he and Zarex stepped slowly around the pod, talking with their heads close together.

"I suppose we're dismissed," Danec said uncertainly.

"I hope so," I said, "because I really need a shower and change of clothes. And a hairbrush." My hair must look like a bird's nest had an argument with a squirrel.

"We'll show you to your quarters," one of the security officers said. The way he looked at me suggested we weren't trusted yet. I was too tired to think why, or what it might mean. I just nodded, took Danec's hand, and followed them out the door.

Before it closed behind us, I glanced back to see Zarex's eyes squarely at me. He looked away the moment he saw me notice.

I shrugged it off as nothing. To Slek, I gave a smile and a wave, then the door closed between us.

"It's not far." Both of the security officers were Parvoran. In spite of their lack of smiles, they both seemed friendlier than J'avet. It must be just him then, who was a grumpy pants.

I rubbed my weary brow with the tip of my fingers and said, "I've never seen a female Parvoran. Are there any?" That sounded rude, even to my ears, but I was tired and my diplomacy needed a polish as much as I did.

"There are many," one of them said. He had a pleasant face, like he smiled often. "They remain on Parvora."

"All of them?" I asked in surprise.

"Yes indeed." He had clearly fielded this question before. "As is their place."

"Oh. I see." Was that why J'avet didn't like me? Because I hadn't stayed home? I smirked to myself. If that was the case, he was shit out of luck. I still planned to go to Agus and continue my study. Nothing he said or did could change that.

"They prefer it that way," the other guard added. "Fewer men to inconvenience them."

"Right." I was sure some of them would agree.

Goodness knows plenty of human women have wanted just that since the dawn of time, but plenty didn't. Men, after all, have cocks. Those come in handy from time to time.

The security officers exchanged glances, but neither seemed bothered by my response. It was their culture, they could live it however they wanted, but I wasn't my cup of tea.

We stopped in front of a set of doors which slid open at the press of a button on the wall.

"You're free to come and go, but we'll accompany you until the captain says otherwise," one of the officers said. "It's just a precaution after what happened with *Infinity* and *Artemis*."

Was that the name of the ship the rogues destroyed, which sent chunks raining down on Calig? I spared a thought for her crew, caught up in an old war that had nothing to do with them.

I nodded. "Fine. We only plan to rest."

The officer nodded. "I'll have food sent."

We stepped inside and the door closed behind us.

The room we were in was as small as one might expect on a ship. Down one side were cubicles, each containing a bed and set of drawers. Down the other was a table and a long bench under the wide window. A door to the rear led to a bathroom, with four shower stalls and four unisex toilets. Two sinks occupied a space in the corner. Beside that was a set of shelves full of clothing, with the size marked on each shelf.

A quick glance showed they even had my size.

"I'm going to have a shower," I said. I hesitated for a moment before I added, "Do you want to join me?" With a trembling hand, I laced my little finger in his.

Danec's eyes lit up like all of his festive celebrations had come as once. "Yes," he said immediately. His face turned darker blue. "I mean, that would be great."

"Great," I said too. Suddenly shy, I turned my back, stepped into a shower cubicle and stripped off my clothes.

He followed me in and closed and locked the door behind us.

I heard him undress and saw his clothes join mine in a pile on the floor. Without turning around, I waved my palm over the sensor to start the water.

Always warm straight away, the spray on my skin made me sigh.

"That feels so good," I said.

"You look so good," Danec said.

I turned slowly then, to face him.

He was trim and lean in the waist and hips. His stomach was flat under the washboard lines of his abs. A perfect V slanted down toward a cock bigger than I had expected.

"Wow." I grabbed the bar of soap and started to wash my arm.

"Wow?" He took the soap and turned me gently so he could run it over my back.

"Yes." I pulled my hair up out of the way. "You're hot. Mmmm, and you have great hands."

"Thank you." He leaned in and kissed the back of my neck. He kissed around to the side and let his tongue flick across the point just under my jaw. "You taste good."

He wound a hand around me and ran the soap over my breasts, first one, then the other. From there, he moved down my belly.

I shivered with the deliciousness of his touch. This felt so decadent and right. His touch was light, gentle, but erotic at the same time. My exhaustion wasn't gone, but I put it aside in favour of quickly growing desire.

"It's my turn." I took the soap from him and turned him so I could lather his back. I started at his muscular shoulders and worked down slowly. I took my time with the firm cheeks of his ass.

He gave it a playful wiggle.

I giggled and moved the soap over his hips and around to his rock hard belly.

"All right, turn around." I soaped up my hands and placed the bar back on the shelf.

Danec turned, but I saw him swallow. He knew what was coming and so did his cock, which was half erect already.

I gripped it carefully in my hands and rubbed my fingers up and down until his length was slick with lather. I worked it a bit more firmly, as his cock hardened more. The water washed the soap away until there was nothing under my hands but wet cock.

The more I worked him, the more individual bumps rose on his cock. Those bumps became nodules the size of a pebble, like a handheld massager, or pearls.

Holy fuck, how would he feel inside me?

While I worked, his hands wandered all over my body, caressing here and stroking there. He brushed over my nipples, down my belly to my other curls.

His hand slid between my legs and grazed against the front of my folds.

I shifted one foot enough to part my legs a little more.

He slipped his hand in further and brushed against my clit.

I whimpered as even that small touch sent bolts of desire arcing through me.

"Danec," I said breathlessly. "I want you."

He silenced me with a kiss as sweet as it was wet with water from the shower.

He pulled back and spoke with a husky voice, "I want you too."

I worked his cock until his eyelids fluttered shut and his hips bucked against my hand.

Before he could come, he drew himself out of my hands and knelt down in front of me. Gently, he parted my legs and pressed his face between them.

I propped my foot on the seat to the side of the shower to give him better access.

His tongue, split in two, flicked lightly against my folds. Then firmer as his confidence grew. Both sides licked my clit, tickling and teasing. He must have pulled both sides of his tongue together, because in the next moment his touch was firm, hard, the texture licking insistently while his lips sucked all around me.

I arched my back and let the water wash down

over me, while an orgasm built inside me. Every flick, every lick, every suck drove me higher and higher, closer and closer. This was more than just pleasure, it was intimacy between two people who cared for each other. Who had been through an ordeal and survived.

Every moment showed how we felt about each other. I trusted him with all of my intimate places, inside and out.

"Danec," I breathed. I moaned so loudly the whole ship might hear, if the walls weren't thick enough to keep in the sound. "Yes…" I cried out as I came, hard and fast, my body rocking, grinding against his mouth.

He licked me until every last drop of orgasm drained out of my body and washed down the drain. Then he stood.

I caught my breath, but didn't hesitate to pull him to me, so his cock was against my entrance, bumps and all. I pushed my hips forward, onto his tip.

"Oh." His tongue darted over his lips. "Are you sure?"

I wasn't sure how much more I could do to declare my certainty, but I whispered, "Yes. Please."

He blew out a breath and eased his cock inside me. His bumps rubbed against my clit as he slid in and slowly out again. The friction felt incredible and made me horny all over again.

I quivered and tilted my hips forward to take him in deeper.

The nodules on his cock rubbed their way up my insides. They created a flood of sensation like pops of electricity that sent pleasure all the way up to my belly.

"Oh my goodness," I breathed.

He froze. "Are you all right?"

"Better than all right," I said. So, so all right.

"Great," he exhaled a ragged breath.

I fought back a smile and reached around to cup his hard ass. Damn, how did I get so lucky?

He drew out, then slid back in deeper. Each thrust massaged me inside and out. Another orgasm grew faster than I ever would have thought possible. I may never get enough of this, enough of him.

He placed his hands on the wall to either side of me and closed his eyes as he thrust harder and harder.

"You feel great," he said softly. "I mean, amazing."

I smiled. "You feel pretty amazing yourself." The last word trailed off into a moan. My fingernails dug into his ass.

He leaned down to graze his teeth over my shoulder, then bit hard enough to leave a mark.

I groaned louder.

He bit harder. Not enough to draw blood, but enough to drive me wild. His teeth would leave marks to match the ones on my breasts from Slek.

The thought pushed me to the edge and over, into an orgasm so intense it bordered on painful, but in the best way possible.

Danec grunted and paused mid-thrust to grunt again as he came, buried deep inside me. He ground his hips against me, his breath in ragged pants. Just when I thought he would sag, he grunted again, louder this time and ground harder still. He bit down on my shoulder and cried out against my flesh as he came again.

Oh my.

Finally, he gasped and his body sagged, his face pressed against my shoulder. His weight bore us both down to the seat, where we half sat, half leaned, still entangled, his cock still deep inside me.

"Wow," I said.

"Wow is right." He pulled out of me and we got more comfortable. He put his arms around me and held me close.

We stayed like that until my eyes started to close.

"We should get dry," I said reluctantly.

"Let me," Danec said. He rose, turned off the water, and reached for the towel, which hung on a hook on the back of the door. He tugged me gently to my feet and started to dry me, first my face and hair, then moving down slowly. He lingered at my breasts and ass, but soon worked his way down to my feet.

"Thank you." I took the towel from him as he rose and wrapped it around my hair before I grabbed a dry one and started on him.

"Hey, where are you guys? There's food here." Slek's voice startled me.

"Coming," I called out. I shared a smile with Danec. We had both done our share of coming already, but this time involved food. I was okay with that.

I wrapped one towel around Danec's hips and pulled the one off my hair to pull around myself.

Danec opened the door and stepped outside. I followed a moment later.

Slek, who stood in the bedroom, a sandwich halfway to his mouth, gave Danec a look of envy, but he was clearly impressed. "There you two are. I see you missed me." He grinned.

I rolled my eyes and found some clean clothes to

pull on. I chose a big t-shirt and some soft shorts.

Danec only grabbed some track pants.

"So what did the IF want?" I stepped into the bedroom and started to work my hair dry.

"They wanted to see how I rigged the cannon to the pod, and asked what I knew about *Infinity*. They think..." Slek paused for effect, "I was pushed."

"I keep telling you that's what happened," I said, only half joking.

Slek shrugged. "The problem is, there are more rogues out there. More Iri too. They aren't going to stop trying to kill each other, and other people are going to get caught in the middle."

I walked to the tray of food on the table and snagged a sandwich and a cup of water.

"There's more," Slek said. "IF is sending me to Agus to teach other engineers my cannon trick."

I stopped, mid-chew. "You're coming to Agus too?" I swallowed hastily and grinned.

He grinned too. "Yes, we're all going. And with any luck, coming."

I laughed.

Danec blushed, but managed a laugh as well. "That's great, we can take care of each other."

"Yes, us and Brinley," I said tired but happy. "We make a good team."

Slek raised his cup at me. "A very good team.

Danec added his cup to the toast. "A great team."

I laughed and threw a piece of sandwich at him.

He caught it and when I thought he might eat it, he placed it into my mouth instead.

I smiled around it while I chewed.

"An awesome team," Danec said softly. "Will that make it harder to choose?"

I grimaced. That might make it impossible to choose, but I had a feeling I was going to have a good time, in the meantime. I eyed Slek's groin speculatively. I was satisfied for now, but I was curious how he would feel. Some ridiculous part of me was still curious how J'avet would feel. It was probably professional curiosity. I was supposed to learn about alien physiology after all. Maybe I could write a book. Or I could focus on getting to know the two incredible guys right in front of me.

The future was going to be interesting.

THE PARTICLES FLOATED THROUGH SPACE. Some nanobots found others and they joined up, like their programming dictated. They floated past debris, crawled over it and cannibalised as much material as they could use.

The swarm grew.

Floated on.

Toward the shipping lanes.

Uh-o, that can't be good. Find out what happens next in Star Defenders.

ABOUT THE AUTHOR

Maggie Alabaster writes reverse harem and, paranormal, sci-fi and fantasy romance.

She lives in NSW, Australia with one spouse, two daughters, one dog, and countless birds.

Sign up for my newsletter! Sign Up!

Join my reader group! Join here!

Follow me on Bookbub! Click here to follow me!

Check out my website- www.maggiealabaster.com

ALSO BY MAGGIE ALABASTER

Dark Masque

Book 1 Bait

Book 2 Prey

Book 3 Trap

Saving Abbie

Book 1 Pitch

Book 2 Pound

Book 3 Session

Book 4 Muse

Book 5 Rhythm

Book 6 Encore

Novella Venomous

Ruthless Claws

Book 1 Ivory

Book 2 Crimson

Book 3 Elodie

Harmony's Magic

Book 1 Summoned by Fire

Book 2 Summoned by Fate

Book 3 Summoned by Desire

Shifter's Vault

Book 1 Discarded

Book 2 Deceived

Book 3 Disgraced

My Alien Mates

Book 1 Star Warriors

Book 2 Star Defenders

Book 3 Star Protectors

Academy of Modern Magic

Book 1 Digital Magic

Book 2 Virtual Magic

Book 3 Logical Magic

Complete Collection

Summer's Harem

Book 1: Shimmer

Book 2: Glimmer

Book 3: Flicker

Complete collection

www.ingramcontent.com/pod-product-compliance
Lightning Source LLC
Chambersburg PA
CBHW020509120726
47904CB00003B/758